DISCARD

# The
# FRIENDSHIP
# EXPERIMENT

# The
# FRIENDSHIP
# EXPERIMENT

## ERIN TEAGAN

HOUGHTON MIFFLIN HARCOURT

BOSTON NEW YORK

The text was set in 12 pt. Chaparral Pro.

Library of Congress Cataloging-in-Publication Data is available.
ISBN 978-0-544-63622-4

Manufactured in the United States of America
DOC 10 9 8 7 6 5 4 3 2 1
4500615285

# one

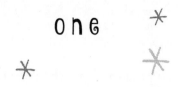

"LOOK, MADELINE." Brooke holds up a pair of weird scissors. "For your nose hairs," she says, about three times louder than necessary.

I yank them out of her hand and throw them back onto the pile of junk. "You're such a newborn," I say. Who's going to buy a pair of used nose-hair clippers? I lean over and write FREE on the tag, then reach for a silvery, rusted contraption with a one-fingered handle. One of Grandpa's secret scientific instruments? It squeaks as I open and close it.

"It's an eyelash curler, dummy."

I toss it back onto the folding table set up in Grandpa's living room. What in the world was my famous scientist grandfather doing with an eyelash curler?

"I'm not a dummy." Even though I'm the younger sister, I'm the one who inherited all the family genius. I point to a cracked bowl. "If you're so smart, what's this?"

Brooke smiles. "Fingernail bath. Do I have to teach you everything?"

"It's called a crucible. For science experiments," I say, tightening my ponytail. "Can you say *cah-ru-ci-ble*?"

"This is boring. I'm going outside with Dad." Brooke flounces out the door to the patio tables for sale in the front yard.

I rifle through the stuff on the table one more time, just to make sure I haven't missed something. My plastic bag is already bulging with Grandpa's unused Eppendorf tubes and an ancient-looking tong that was probably instrumental in at least one of his scientific discoveries. From underneath an old magazine I grab a timer that looks like an amoeba and then take my seat behind the table, watching strangers walk in and out of Grandpa's house.

I can't get used to the idea of this estate sale. All these people, touching all of Grandpa's stuff, pulling things off shelves, dismantling beds and carrying them off to who knows where. Probably a good thing Grandpa's not alive to see this.

My stomach throbs.

"Does this still work?" A girl stands in front of me, wearing a shirt that says $e=mc^2$.

I can't believe what she's holding in her hand. "Where'd

you get that? Not for sale," I say, taking the gold clock away from her. She probably took it right off Grandpa's desk, the little thief. It even has his name on the base from when he retired: DR. LEONARD LITTLE, BIOCHEMIST. There's no way Dad would sell this, right?

She's holding a bag of gummy bears in her other hand, and now she's looking over the table and pushing things around. Her fingers are probably sticky.

I stand up. "Most of these things are not for sale, actually." I don't know what I'm saying. I look over my shoulder at Mom, who is busy picking through Grandpa's books by the fireplace.

"Really?" The girl stops chewing. "Even these things with price tags?"

"Two-minute rule," I say, starting my amoeba timer. "Two minutes to look around, and that's it. You know, for sanitary reasons."

The girl laughs like I'm making a joke, and I want to push the whole table over.

"I'm Riley," she says. "We just moved here. Gummy bear?" She has a whole armful of bracelets that clink as she holds out the bag. I shake my head. She holds up a plastic beaker with a burn hole in the bottom. "Okay. I'll just buy this, then. Need it for my experiments."

"Making a volcano?" Because all kids who think

they're scientists make volcanoes and collect rocks, two very unscientific things. I've never collected a rock in my whole life.

"No volcano. I'm really good at experiments," she says. "I love space, too. I just got back from Space Camp."

"The real Space Camp?" The one I've begged to go to for my entire existence?

She pops another gummy bear into her mouth. "Of course. I'm going to be an astronaut." This girl sure knows how to brag.

"My birthday is on Astronomy Day this year." I'm blinking way too fast. I take a breath and see she's still holding Grandpa's beaker. "Well, that'll be one thousand dollars."

"It says ten cents." She points at the price tag.

Mom and Dad are going to notice I'm not selling anything. That I keep putting things in my own bag. Even though I already have a science collection pouring out of my closet and creeping out from under my bed.

"It's like ten cents times ten thousand, actually."

More people are filtering into the house now. Through the open front door I can see shoppers outside trying out the camping chairs and dipping their hands in the fountain that's for sale. Brooke's best friend is there, and

I wonder where my own best friend is. Or maybe Elizabeth's too busy with her new fancy summer reading list for her new fancy private school, New Hope. It will be my first day at plain old Jasper Johns Middle School tomorrow. Home of the Mighty Barn Owls. Hoot! Hoot!

My stomach has gone from throbbing to churning. Riley is still staring at me. "Are you all right?" she says.

I fan myself with a *Scientist Today* magazine, trying to breathe the fresh air coming in through the front door. One of Grandpa's standard operating procedures is still taped to the old wall phone nearby.

> *How to Call Your Son.*
>
> *Step 1. Pick up the receiver, which is the blue handle-looking thing with a spirally cord.*
>
> *Step 2. Dial 5-5-5-0-2-0-4 in that exact order.*
>
> *Step 3. Tell your son to buy his daughter a telescope.*

(I wrote that last step.)

If anyone needs a standard operating procedure right now, it's me. I make up my own SOP in my head: *How to Get Rid of Someone.*

*Step 1. Casually mention a horrifying and terrible disease.*

"We just got back from South Africa," I say, straightening up and folding my arms across my chest. "Really sad about that bubonic plague there."

"South Africa doesn't have the plague," she says. "Nobody does."

"It kills just about everyone. We were probably exposed."

*Step 2. Cough loudly. Do not cover your mouth.*

Mom is over by the fireplace. "You okay, Madeline?"

*Step 3. Excuse yourself to the hospital.*

"It's like the most contagious disease on record. Maybe I should go to the emergency room." I cough again.

Riley looks unconvinced. "If you really had the bubonic plague, your body parts would start turning black, and you'd have red bumps all over you." She puts the beaker on the table.

Red. Like blood. My blood is actually feeling too hot, filling my fingertips and pulsing in my ears.

"Anyway," she's saying, "I don't have a thousand dollars for a used beaker. Maybe I'll see you in school tomorrow." She leaves through the front door and I stand at the table for a good ten seconds before I feel sick for real. My stomach lurches and the room spins.

I wipe my nose, then grab the burned-out beaker and hold it to my chest, expecting to smell the lab in it. But it only smells like melted plastic and char. And then I grab three more beakers, the crucible, a Bunsen burner with a frayed gas line, two funnels, and a pack of unused petri dishes. I sit in my chair, my arms so full I can barely see over my loot, until Dad comes, feeling my forehead and peeling my hands apart, making me put everything back on the table.

"How about a break? You don't want to overdo it. Come on," he says, and tries to smile.

I follow Dad, who gets me a glass of ice water from the kitchen and then heads up the stairs. Everything's feeling wrong and backward somehow. There's a painting propped up against the wall, and I hang it back up where it belongs. In the bedrooms there are more shoppers circling Grandpa's treasures.

I wish more than anything that there was an SOP for all of this. A simple three-step procedure that would fix everything. Grandpa would know how to write it. But now that he's gone, it's up to me.

# TWO

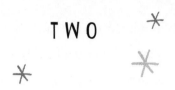

THE ONLY room in the house that is off-limits for the estate sale is Grandpa's attic study. Dad leads me up the stairs, my body still hot even though I'm holding the cold glass in my hand.

"You can lie down here, Madeline," Dad says. When he swings the door open, the smell of Grandpa — hand sanitizer and barbecue potato chips — rolls over me. I take a gulp of water.

Dad clears his throat. "Haven't been up here to go through things yet."

I flop onto the dimpled leather couch by the small round window that looks out over the university campus and the research hospital. Dad and Grandpa worked in the same lab there, researching the bleeding disorder that runs in my family, Von Willebrand disease.

Mom flip-flops up the stairs. "Are you okay, Maddie?" She rushes over and touches my forehead. "No fever. It's getting awfully stuffy downstairs with all the people.

Good idea to take a break up here for a bit." She pushes wisps of hair away from my face. "I saw you talking to that girl. New friend?"

"Definitely not," I say.

Mom grabs an empty box from the floor and heads over to Grandpa's desk. "You need to open yourself up to friendship, Maddie. Elizabeth won't be with you in school anymore. Where is she, by the way? I thought she'd be here today."

I close my eyes and write another SOP in my head: *How to Fake Sleep to Get Out of a Discussion with Your Mother About Your Social Life.*

*Step 1. Yawn and then go limp. Like complete and total limpness.*

*Step 2. Open your mouth and breathe like you have a nasal blockage.*

*Step 3. If you are on a couch, or a bed, or a chair, dangle an arm or leg off the side for extra effect.*

"Wow," I hear Mom say. "She's out."

Thank you, Grandpa. These SOPs are genius.

I try to ignore Mom and Dad's whisper-talking about selling this house and where to donate everything that's left after the estate sale. And then they have to get back downstairs since they put Brooke in charge, and I hear Mom talking to Dad on the way down about how she wishes I weren't taking all of this so hard. How she thinks everything would be better if I spent less time in my closet laboratory and more time with the rest of the almost-teenagers.

As soon as they're gone, I roll off the couch onto the floor. I bet my parents haven't yet gone into Grandpa's little art studio behind the wall, and I crawl over to the door, which is only half-size because the ceilings up here are slanted. There's paint on the doorknob and a smudge of green underneath. Grandpa's fingerprint.

The paint smell inside is strong, wet and earthy. Grandpa always said the best scientists were also artists, using all parts of the brain. I maneuver around the stacked canvases and find that some of the paint jars are still open. Green and purple and blue. Paintbrushes are soaking in a cup of gray water.

Grandpa had said he wasn't painting anymore because of his arthritis. But then I see his I'M A FUNGI! mug next to the easel, still half-full of his favorite tea, mold creeping over the surface. I peer around the easel and see a half-finished, twisty-turny splatter of paint in the middle of a canvas. It looks almost like a molecule.

Grandpa *was* painting—but he never got to finish this one. My body aches with the plague feeling again and the smell of old tea and paint jars makes the room tilt. I

crawl back out into the attic study and close the door behind me.

I rush down the stairs and out the front door, des-
perate for Elizabeth to be here. I need to show her the
painting and the books and the view from the attic. Just
once more. Because if there is anyone in this whole universe who appreciates the view from up here as much as
Grandpa and I, it's my best friend.

# THree

**B**ROOKE AND ABBY are sitting on matching camping chairs by the fountain. I scan for Elizabeth, then droop into a chair next to Brooke, spilling my bag of loot onto the ground. "Aren't you supposed to be helping?" I say. "Who's manning the trinket table?"

Brooke's eyes are closed, her face in the sun. "Eliza-death was just looking for you."

I perk up. "It's Eliza*beth*. Stop calling her that."

It's possible that Elizabeth is a little bossy. And maybe sometimes she thinks she's the smartest person on the planet. But she's not boring, like Brooke thinks she is. For one thing, she has her own telescope. Pointed to Mars. In her bedroom. "Where'd she go?"

Brooke points a lazy finger at the lawn mower and beach umbrellas. I walk over, my bag swinging on my arm. See? I have friends. I am so well-rounded it's ridiculous. If Space Camp gave free tuition to kids based on their well-roundedness, I'd be the first recipient.

I find Elizabeth digging in her backpack under a fluorescent beach umbrella, a row of pencils on the ground.

"Cool pencils," I say.

"I have a new smiley-face one for you, but I can't find it. I figure you need it more than ever for good luck on your first day as a Barn Owl."

Elizabeth and I have the same appreciation for a good writing utensil. She pulls out a puppy-love pencil and tosses it to the ground. I shuffle through my bag too, feeling generous. I pull out a pen made to look like a pipette, blue with rotating numbers. "Here. I got this for you."

Elizabeth looks up. "Awesome. I can keep this?"

Some guy leans in to look at the price tag on the beach umbrella. "Not for sale," I say, ripping the tag right off the metal spindles. He gives me the stink-eye and moves to a blanket scattered with stuff under the next beach umbrella.

"Why'd you do that?" Elizabeth says.

I change the subject. "Want to come see the attic one last time?" Bubonic plague throbs in my throat, but I swallow it down, collect my things, and crawl out from under the umbrella.

Elizabeth follows me. "Don't say that."

But we know it's true — one last time. Grandpa may

have been the best scientist in the world, but he wasn't so great at keeping up this old house, even with Mom and Dad's help. Dad says we'd have to gut the place to live in it, and we can't afford that. So now we have to sell it to some family that probably doesn't even know a famous scientist lived here.

We weave through the throng of people going through the drawers in the kitchen and tread back up to the attic.

Elizabeth stops at the top of the stairs and looks around at Grandpa's office. I look at my shoes. She pulls me across the creaking floor and picks up the miniature globe that is also a pencil sharpener from Grandpa's top shelf.

"You can have that," I say.

Elizabeth smiles at me. "Thanks."

I lean down, looking at a row of books on the bottom shelf. They're blank. Old lab notebooks that were never used. I take the oldest-looking one, the edges yellowed, and open the front cover. Grandpa's name is scribbled inside: *Leonard Little, Dept. of Hematology.*

"There are only twenty sixth-graders at my new school," Elizabeth says. "Just twenty."

There will be about one million three thousand sixth-graders at Jasper Johns Middle School tomorrow. Way more than at our elementary school. And probably most of them don't even know the difference between an alligator and a crocodile.

"I wish you could come with me," she says.

"Me too." I just can't believe the injustice of it all. Why does my life have to be ruined because my mother supports public education?

"At least you'll know some people from our old school at Jasper Johns," Elizabeth says. "It's better than not knowing anyone, right?" She jiggles her globe, tiny pencil shavings falling to the floor.

I add the lab notebook to my bag of science stuff. "Maybe." And we start back down the stairs, Elizabeth taking one last look over her shoulder at Grandpa's attic office.

Downstairs a little kid is poking his sister with Grandpa's magnifying glass, which is breakable and delicate and should probably be in a museum somewhere. I want to snatch it right out of his fist, but Elizabeth pushes me out the door and back to the fountain, where Brooke and Abby are still sunbathing.

"I have to go," Elizabeth says. "I still have three chapters of *Watership Down* to finish for summer reading. And then I have to get ready for school. My mom's making me go to bed at like eight o'clock."

The side door of the house swings open and Mom

bustles out, maneuvering a large canvas. "What is that?" I say. The painting is huge, with bright colors and a fancy frame. Definitely not one of Grandpa's.

"I found it in the front closet!" Mom says, red splotches all over her face, the way she gets when something exciting happens. Like that time when Earth Love had their going-out-of-business sale and all organic cotton underwear was 75 percent off. She was splotched for three days straight. "It was in a stack of Monet and Van Gogh reproductions. Hidden, like a treasure!"

She props the painting against the edge of the fountain and steps back to admire it. Brooke leaps out of her chair, her face full of horror. "Ick!" For once, we agree on something.

The brushstrokes are thick and blurred, but you can tell the lady sitting on an old-fashioned sofa is nearly-almost naked, except for a silky draped scarf.

"Is it gone yet?" Brooke says. She and Abby are hiding their faces.

"I knew your grandfather had an eye for art," Mom says, clapping. "I've seen this somewhere before. Maybe when we were in Italy?"

"It's very nice, Mrs. Little," Elizabeth says, her eyes averted.

Brooke peeks around her hands just long enough to say, "I swear if you bring that home I'm running away."

"Such a powerful message." Mom shakes her head, staring at the painting. "What do you think, girls? Materialism or the quest for transparency?"

Elizabeth nudges me. "Good luck tomorrow." And she bolts across the front lawn, practically leaping over the recycling bins.

I'm watching her half running down the sidewalk toward campus when I spot the middle school soccer team jogging up the road toward us. They're practically famous, winning districts almost every year. Brooke has their team picture hanging on her wall. I yell, "Hoot! Hoo—"

Brooke nearly tackles me. I drop my science stuff, and my Eppendorf tubes roll all over the grass. "Hey, you just made me—" Before I can finish, Brooke clamps her hand over my mouth.

I make up an SOP in my head, super fast: *How to Get Someone's Hand off Your Mouth.*

*Step 1. Lick the hand.*

Brooke flies back. "Did you just lick me?"

I don't even have to think of a Step 2.

"Be quiet! They're going to look over here!" she whispers, her eyes darting to the captain, who is leading the pack: Dexter Sully, the not-so-secret love of Brooke's life. I stuff all the tubes back into the bag and retrieve my lab notebook from under a bush.

"I have barely any makeup on!" Brooke cries, ripping her ponytail out and fluffing her hair.

"I didn't even dry my hair this morning," Abby says, cowering next to her.

The soccer team is running past Grandpa's driveway, and some of the players are waving. I wave back and shout, "Hoot! Hoot!"

"Stop it!" Brooke hisses. She's the one who told me in the first place that we're supposed to *Hoot! Hoot!* whenever we see any player from our school. It's tradition. It's team spirit. Yet I start to see why she might be upset. Maybe sitting with your mom and little sister on camping chairs from the sixties with an inappropriate painting propped up behind you isn't the best situation. Not to mention that Mom's wearing an organic burlap dress with a matching headband she made while on safari in Africa about twenty years ago, which is embarrassing enough.

"My life is over," Brooke whimpers.

"They're gone," Abby says, which is for the most part true. Some of them are still craning their necks for one more look at Mom's painting.

As soon as they round the corner, Brooke loses all composure. "He was laughing! Did you see him laughing?" She turns on me. "Look what you did! How will he — they — take me seriously as a cheerleader when they all know I come from a totally weird family that has paintings of naked ladies?"

"I'm sure Dexter wasn't laughing at you, Brooke," Abby says.

"Yes, he was." She flaps her hands to her sides. "And the Pumpkin Tournament is only a few weeks away." That's when the soccer players give their jerseys to the eighth-grade cheerleaders, who wear them everywhere for the rest of the year. Stinky. Grass-stained. Like a badge of cheerleading honor.

"You'll still get a jersey. Don't worry," I say helpfully.

"She doesn't want just anyone's jersey, Maddie," Abby says.

Brooke rolls her eyes. "Seriously, Maddie, you are so clueless. How are we even related? Mom, can we please go now?"

"Where's Dad?" I say, looking around.

"He's going to close things up here and check in at the lab," Mom says.

I don't even ask if I can go with him. Ever since they

had that concentrated acid spill, Mom doesn't like me going to the lab.

"Who's going to help me carry this thing all the way home?" Mom says, brushing a grass clipping from the canvas.

Brooke's saying goodbye to Abby, so I hold up my bag and notebook. "I'm already carrying this and this."

"All right, Brooke, grab a corner!" Mom says.

Brooke straightens. "What? Me?"

Mom pats the top of the painting. "Come on, Muscles."

Brooke pinches my arm as I hurry past her and then we're off: my mom, my sister, the naked lady, and I, marching across the lawn.

I pick up my pace, putting some distance between us in case Mom declares Brooke inadequate and makes me take her place. We'll practically pass the science museum on the way home, so I speed up even more. "I need to stop at the museum, okay?" I call over my shoulder.

It's more than a museum, really. They have a three-dimensional model of the human brain in the lobby, their own planetarium, and a high school science club that gets to make medicine out of tree sap. I've been a member since I was six, and every year for my birthday Mom and Dad let me pick something out at the gift shop. This year is different, though. Elizabeth and I want tickets to the science museum's once-in-a-lifetime Snoozatarium. We'll sleep under the stars in their planetarium. On Astronomy Day. Which is also my birthday.

There's just one problem. It's sold out.

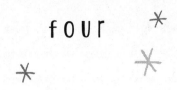

# four

WHEN I SWING the museum's door open, a whoosh of cool air hits me. I could easily live in this place. Just bring my solar system sleeping bag and cozy up with the wax statue of Marie Curie on the third floor. I wonder if anyone would notice.

"Afternoon, Maddie," Kevin says from behind the front desk. He's holding out a plate of astronaut ice cream. "Straight out of the food lab."

I take a cube of strawberry and pop the entire glorious thing into my mouth.

"Tickets for the Snoozatarium are still sold out," Kevin says, helping himself to a chunk of chocolate. "If that's why you're here."

"That's my birthday, you know." Honestly, how many people get the chance to have a sleepover in the planetarium on their actual birthday that is also Astronomy Day? I cross my arms. "My dad really meant to buy tickets, but he's been super busy."

Kevin nods and hands me another strawberry ice cream cube. "They sold out in the first hour."

"But I've been a member of this place since I was six! You should have warned me that could happen."

"Sorry, Maddie. If it were up to me, I'd give you a ticket."

I scramble to think up an SOP on *How to Deal with Someone Who's Totally Unfair*.

*Step 1. Tell the person of unfairness that their behavior is unacceptable and you'll have to report them to the person in charge.*

*Step 2. And that they should look up the definition of unfairness and read it a lot of times.*

*Step 3. And you hope their astronaut ice cream is rotten.*

"I'll let you know, though, Maddie. We've got you on the waiting list." Kevin scrolls through something on his computer. "Number twelve." He smirks.

"It is not nice to lie to kids, you know." Twelve is how old I'll be on my birthday. A fact I may have shared a time or two.

"All right, all right. You're number twenty-three." Twenty-three means there is basically no possible way I'll be at the Snoozatarium. They're even letting people in the zero gravity room in their pajamas. The lack of justice in this world is killing me.

There's a knock on the giant plate glass window by the door, and it's Mom. She's drawn a small crowd with her inappropriate painting, and Brooke is stretched out on the low wall by the willow tree. She's dabbing at her face and I stop, wondering if she's getting a bloody nose. The crowd of ladies by the painting moves in my sister's direction as Brooke sits up, then leaps to stand to save her shirt from the gush of blood. She's been getting these nosebleeds a lot lately.

"Does she need something?" Kevin asks.

"A roll of paper towels? Some ice?" I want to add a doctor or maybe even an ambulance to the list, because sometimes I think her bloody noses might last forever. What if they did? What would happen? I wipe at my own nose — something I do all the time now.

By the time I'm outside armed with paper towels and ice, Brooke is sitting up on the low wall, Mom squeezing the bridge of her nose. The ladies crowd around, trying to help. Mom waves me over. Holding Brooke's hair is my job in these situations. I pat her head so she knows it's me and it's going to be okay, but she flaps a hand at me and yells, "Stop!"

It's hard to put ice on a nose while it's gushing blood and being pinched at the same time, but Mom manages it. The ladies want to call an ambulance, but my mom and

I can tell it's already getting better. Eventually Brooke needs fewer paper towels and then, finally, the blood stops. The ladies walk away after patting Brooke's shoulders, cautious, like they're walking away from a kid on a tightrope over a lion's den. That's usually the first impression Brooke makes when she has an episode.

"Get off!" Brooke says, pulling her hair from my grip.

I step back and give her a dirty look. "You're welcome."

"Time?" Mom says. "Maddie, did you time it?"

I look at my watch. "Five hundred and forty-three seconds."

"In minutes, Madeline."

Brooke stands up, brushing her shorts off and inspecting her silk shirt, which is pretty well ruined. She lets out a wail and Mom gets out her stain stick, dabbing and fretting.

"Nine minutes and three seconds," I say. "One minute, four seconds longer than the last one."

Mom steps back and gives Brooke a meaningful look. It's the *a few more of these and you're going to the doctor* look.

"It's the first day of school tomorrow," Brooke pleads. "Can I still meet Abby at Pizza Palace later?"

And I remember how last year we all met at Pizza Palace the night before school started, and Mom, Dad, and Grandpa sat in one booth and Elizabeth and I sat together

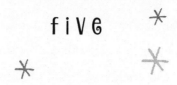

# fiVe

B Y THE TIME we make it to our little neighborhood, Brooke has almost walked into the path of a bike,
tripped me three times, and nearly taken out a toddler, all
while inspecting her swollen face in a mini mirror from
Mom's purse. I'm carrying the naked lady with Mom now,
my bag of science stuff swinging from my elbow. As we
round the corner onto our street, I think I've never been
so happy to see our cul-de-sac in my life.

Mr. Sid is on his front porch, sitting in his favorite
worn-out rocking chair. When we get to our front gate, he
puts his tea down and stares at the naked lady. "What is
this?"

I drop my half of the painting into the grass and shake
out my aching arms.

"Beautiful, right?" Mom says, getting her breath back.
"Just found it. Do you recognize it?"

Mr. Sid shakes his head, moving around the painting.

"It is beautiful, though." He's a retired art professor from the university who now spends all his time in his garden. His front yard is one giant patch of flowers, crawling all the way up to the sidewalk.

Brooke grabs the keys from Mom's purse and lets herself into our house. Slipping past the naked lady admiration club, I follow her and take my bag of science stuff upstairs.

Every time I walk into our bedroom and find Brooke's side empty, I still feel startled. It's been a week since Brooke declared she can't possibly live with me and my science experiments anymore, even though I got rid of the rotten egg floating in vinegar. She moved herself to the cluttered basement laundry room. And I don't miss her one bit. Maybe her panda night-light, but definitely not Brooke and all of her loud singing and stinky nail polish.

I spill my plastic bag onto my bed and re-inspect my new items. The burned-out beaker goes on my bedside table, and I line everything else up on the shelves in the closet. It's pretty cramped in there even with Brooke's stuff gone, but once everything is organized, I sit on my little stool and just admire it all.

There's a stench coming from one of my shelves and I see that a petri dish has gone fuzzy with black and white spots. Last week I swabbed one of Brooke's flip-flops after she wore them to the farm carnival. I had hypothesized that they were going to be completely hazardous and contaminated, and it looks like I was right. I plug my nose and look closer. The plate is still double-taped shut and sealed in a plastic bag, but the smell leaks through anyway. I cough and flick my fan on. Good thing Brooke isn't here to complain.

I take a picture of the dish with one of Grandpa's old lab cameras and tape the thermal paper printout into my microbiology binder under the BROOKE tab. I swab a lot of things — mostly a lot of Brooke's things — because I'm going to be a famous microbiologist. I want to discover every new kind of bacteria and fungus in the world.

When I flip open my copy of *Bergey's Manual of Determinative Bacteriology*, I find an illustration that looks just like my plate. It's just regular old fungus. But one day I'm going to find something that nobody has ever seen before.

All the pictures of my petri dishes are in this giant binder, organized and tabbed alphabetically, with special experiments filed in the back. My favorite picture of all time is from when I swabbed the inside of the kitchen trash when we missed garbage pickup after Thanksgiving two years ago. Pink and yellow and white polka dots all over. Grandpa said it looked like a piece of art. Mom threw out the trash can.

When I leave my closet, plugging my nose and holding the foul plastic bag with two fingers, the picture of the Von Willebrand factor on the door of the closet makes me pause. I shut the door for a closer look, and realize it's the same molecule from Grandpa's half-finished painting. Why didn't I think of that before? It's the most important molecule in our family's life. It's the protein that helps people's blood clot. Except our Von Willebrand factor is damaged. It's the reason our blood doesn't clot like it should. The reason Grandma died after Dad was born. The reason people want to alert the authorities when Brooke has an episode. And the reason I wear my medical bracelet.

It was Grandpa's life work to research Von Willebrand disease, and now it will be Dad's, if he can keep his grant money and continue his research. I trace the picture with one finger.

There's barking outside, and when I look out my window on Brooke's side of the room, I see Bark the bulldog in our yard. He lives three doors down, but basically has free reign over the neighborhood. His owner hasn't noticed the bulldog-size holes under her fence. Mr. Sid, who has taken it upon himself to be the guardian of all the gardens on the street, is launching pinecones at Bark from his patio. Bark doesn't even flinch as he does his business in our yard and then lumbers back home.

From the window I can just make out Grandpa's house — the very tiptop of his attic — and the university beyond. I see Dad coming up our street at his normal turbo-fast pace. He swings into the house and I hear his boots on the stairs.

"Hi, Dad!" I call.

He's already halfway down the hall, and he waves to me over his shoulder. But I only have to wait for a second until he has what he needs and spins back around toward the stairs. "He's acting up again," Dad says, a wrench in his hand.

"He" is the autoclave at the lab. A massive sterilizer with a mind of his own. Basically, he's a giant robot dishwasher. An old, crabby, robot dishwasher. Dad says if there were any money left in their budget, he'd get a new autoclave in a second.

"You don't have a wrench at the lab?"

"The guys over in Fermentation probably stole it again," he says.

"If we moved into Grandpa's house, you could keep

your tools in a garage instead of under your bed," I say, smirking.

He pokes me with the wrench. "Wish that was a good option for us, sweetheart."

I hand him the bagged-up petri dish.

"Oooh, fungus." Dad grimaces. "Nice growth. You take a picture?"

I nod. I'm only allowed to grow stuff on petri dishes if I let Dad take them to the lab to be disposed of properly. And no opening the plates once they're taped shut. Otherwise I could unleash a man-eating bacteria or something.

"I'll be back for dinner," Dad says, and then he spins his wrench and heads down the stairs like he can fix anything in his path.

# SIX

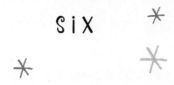

WHEN I GO downstairs the next morning, Mom has already set out breakfast: two plates with cinnamon-raisin French toast, real maple syrup, and a pat of butter in the shape of a star for good luck. A first-day-of-school celebration. Dad went to the lab early, and Mom's sipping her Wake Up! tea in her reading chair, directly next to the naked lady painting, just waiting to be hung.

"Mom." I mean, it's disturbing. There's art, and then there's just a plain old nearly naked person on a canvas.

She pops out of the chair. "There's my middle school girl!"

I don't feel like celebrating. I stand in the center of the room with my arms crossed over Grandpa's lab notebook, which is coming to school with me. How am I supposed to become a genius microbiologist by going to a regular old school that makes square dancing part of the curriculum? Especially when my best friend gets to go to the fancy New Hope School down the road.

I open my notebook and write an SOP on *How to Resist French Toast.*

*Step 1. Picture it with a pile of seaweed salad on top.*

I picture it so well that I gag. "Smells disgusting."

"Sit down." Mom takes the seat at the table next to my plate. "You'll miss the bus."

"I'll walk."

*Step 2. Pretend it's covered in poisonous mold.*

Mom pours the warm, sticky, wonderful syrup over my French toast. "What are you writing? Put that in your backpack and sit down."

And I can't even get to Step 3. My mouth waters against my will and my legs defy me, walking me right over to the table. I am an SOP failure.

I take a sweet, drippy first bite, ignoring Brooke, who has thundered up the stairs from her basement bedroom and is frantically digging through the junk drawer.

Mom stirs her tea, yawning. "Middle school." She nods. "You ready?"

I swallow another bite. "I guess." I've been up for an hour, repacking my backpack, tucking a bunch of swabs into the front zipper pocket, and revising my SOP on *How to Appropriately Excuse Yourself from Class to Use the Facilities.* If I'm forced to go to regular school I'll no doubt be the smartest, most prepared, best scientist of the bunch.

"I gave you an extra scoop of red pepper hummus in your lunchbox, your favorite."

It's Elizabeth's favorite too. We always sat together at lunch. Who will I sit with now?

Mom tugs my ponytail. "I signed up to teach an after-school program."

I push away my plate. "What?"

"Found it!" Brooke shrills from her spot at the junk drawer. She holds up a bottle of red nail polish and pounds past us to the couch.

"What kind of program?" I say, because this is all I need for middle school to be completely and officially ruined.

"No nail polish on the couch, Brooke." Mom slurps her tea. "I don't know yet. Maybe I'll call it something like Recycle Kids or EcoKids or —"

Brooke pops up from the couch. "What is she talking about?"

"Oh, don't worry, I won't embarrass you," Mom says, waving her hand toward Brooke. "I wish my mother had done something like this when I was in school."

I make eye contact with my sister, and for that single moment we're on the same side. Nana would *never* have done something like this when Mom was our age. I picture my mother marching down the halls of our school, wearing an eco-friendly burlap dress with matching beret, a giant bag of eco-friendly paraphernalia dragging behind her.

Mom holds her tea halfway to her mouth, staring at the ceiling, her eyes dreamy. "We'll do crafts and games and sing songs about the earth. Maybe we'll even take a few nature walks through the fields behind the school and look for signs of global warming."

"I swear on my entire wardrobe I'll put myself up for adoption," Brooke says.

I clear my throat and Mom snaps out of it. "Don't worry. I made sure we left two spaces in the program for my two favorite EcoKids!"

"I have cheerleading," Brooke says. "Like every single day after school. And then I have to do my homework. So, as much as I'd like to —"

"I'll have homework too!" I squeak.

"Plenty of time for homework *and* fun, Madeline," Mom says.

"I wish I could be there," Brooke says, grabbing her backpack from the table. "It does sound really, really fun."

And *poof!* It's every sister for herself again. I dump my French toast plate into the sink, put on my backpack, and

am nearly out the door when I remember the most important thing.

I race up the stairs and into my bedroom, grabbing
Elizabeth's old friendship pencil off my desk. It's the size
of my thumb, barely usable anymore, but still my favorite.

# seven

WHEN I SIT in my seat on the bus, as far from my traitor-sister as possible, I realize like a thousand red bricks dropped on my head that Grandpa won't be waving from his attic window when we pass his house.

Summer vacation had just started when Grandpa got really sick and collapsed in his kitchen. Dad said his levels were off. Mom said he missed my grandmother too much for one soul. I said he'd be fine; he just needed his black tea. But I was wrong.

Every school morning he used to sit on the little window seat next to his desk and wave to me as I rode by on the school bus. On my birthday he'd wear a birthday hat. On Halloween, he wore a kitty-cat mask meant for a little kid. I look around the bus, panicked, hoping maybe Brooke realizes that we're going to pass Grandpa's house and he's not going to be there. But Brooke's laughing with Abby like there's nothing wrong in the world. And the

French toast in my belly feels too sweet, and the backpack on my lap too heavy.

We turn a corner and I'm lightheaded. How could I have been so unprepared for this? How could I have forgotten Grandpa so fast?

My throat tightens as we pass the coffee shop. And then we must be driving a hundred miles an hour because we're already at the tennis courts. I try to write an SOP in my head, try to recite the prime numbers or the elements in the periodic table. But I can't think of even one.

"Are you okay?" some girl from across the aisle says.

I wipe my nose and my hand is red. Red has dripped onto my leg. My backpack falls to the floor.

"We have a bloody nose here!" the girl yells to the bus driver.

The bus stops and Brooke is beside me, reciting the same things Mom always says over and over. "It's only a little blood. Nothing to worry about. We'll get you cleaned up. Not to worry."

It's my first bloody nose in so many years, and I try so hard not to cry in front of the whole bus full of kids that my head aches. Brooke whips out a roll of paper towels from her bag and I start the stopwatch. "Only a little blood. Not to worry," she says again.

And it feels like we're pinching my nose for eternity. Brooke has the ice pack from my lunchbox on my nose and it makes my whole body go goosebumps. Someone is holding my ponytail back. "I have a complete change of clothes," Brooke says.

*Her hand must be falling asleep,* I think. She's been standing in the same position for — I look at my watch — two hundred thirteen seconds.

"Should we call Mom? Maybe we should call Mom," Brooke says.

It's like I'm not my real self. I'm dizzy. Floating. This can't be happening. Von Willebrand is Brooke's disease. She's the one who has it bad and bleeds too much. Not me.

The bus driver is standing in the aisle, watching. She looks at me the way everyone always looks at Brooke during an episode. "Can I get anything?" she whispers.

Brooke pulls away the bloody towel and comes in fast with a clean one. She's a pro. I want to lie down but she keeps propping me up. "It's slowing down," she says. "Nothing to worry about."

And then it stops. I look at my watch: eight minutes, forty-three seconds.

"You should get checked out by the nurse," the bus driver says. "You want a pass?"

Brooke shakes her head. "She's okay. No need to call

our mom or anything." She rubs my shoulder. "Unless you want to? Do you want to call Mom?"

I'm still dabbing my nose. "No, it's okay."

"Not to worry," Brooke says, pushing all the towels into a plastic bag. "We'll get you cleaned up."

And then I notice that all along we've been stopped in front of Grandpa's house. I wish that by some miracle he were sitting in his window seat giving me a thumbs-up, telling me everything's going to be okay. But the window is dark and empty, and even on this bus full of kids, I've never felt so dark and empty myself.

# eight

$B$ROOKE HELPS me off the bus when we finally get to school. She's got me by the elbow and is jabbering over her shoulder to Abby about their school schedules and how they're never going to survive without gym together. Then they do their squealy jumpy thing because they might have the same lunch as Dexter. And I know I should be worried about all the looks I'm getting because of my blood-spattered shirt, but I can't get the fog out of my mind.

"No one ever uses this bathroom," Brooke says after we've walked for what feels like an hour, Abby stepping on my heels every five seconds.

I sit on a small bench under the hand dryers and Brooke gives me an orange juice from her backpack. "Where'd you get this?" I say.

"You have to be prepared." She pulls a pair of jeans and a shirt from her backpack. Brooke has enough stuff in there to survive a disaster. "You need to start doing this too. You don't want to walk around like that all day, do you?"

I stand up to see myself in the mirror. My face is swollen and my nose is a giant red—

"Don't look!" Brooke grabs me and sits me back down on the bench. "Wait at least a half-hour before looking in the mirror. Nosebleeds are never pretty." She puts a cold wet towel on my nose, dabbing, while I take a sip of warm orange juice.

"I think the bell's about to ring," Abby says.

"Go without me," Brooke says. "Tell Mr. Fitz that I have girl issues."

Abby tosses her gum into the trash and smears a layer of ChapStick on her lips. "I'll save you a seat," she says. "Feel better, Maddie."

And then I hear the bell. Middle school is starting without me, and everyone has probably already claimed the front row and sharpened their favorite pencils and located the fire exits.

I look under the bench. "Wait. Where's my backpack?"

Brooke grabs me. "You're going to start another nosebleed! You can't bend over like that."

I feel the blood rush to my head and stand up so fast I knock over my orange juice. The pile of clean clothes on my lap falls in a heap at my feet. Brooke snatches the jeans off the tile floor before the orange puddle reaches them. "These are new," she says. "They're like a hundred dollars or something."

"I left my backpack on the bus." My nose throbs with heat. "I need my backpack."

Brooke pushes the clothes into my arms. "You don't need a backpack on the first day of school." She nudges me into a bathroom stall. "Get dressed."

When the door closes I lock it super fast because now I can't stop the tears. Hot, giant, baby-elementary-school tears. I touch my nose and feel relieved when there's no blood. It's like Brooke knows I'm frozen inside my little bathroom stall. "Shirt," she calls. "On."

I have no pencils, no backpack, none of my own clothes. Only Von Willebrand disease.

"Hand me your dirty clothes," Brooke says. "Socks too."

"My socks aren't dirty," I say.

Brooke exhales on the other side of the stall door. "You can't wear giant mom socks with skinny jeans."

"These aren't Mom's socks," I say.

"Don't admit that to anyone, ever," she says. "It's not even cold outside. Take them off."

My feet are freezing on the tiles and I get dressed fast now, thinking of all the foot fungus lurking on this floor, wishing I had my swabs for a sample. The jeans are a little long and the shirt is way too form-fitting, but I come out of the stall anyway. Brooke claps. "You look so cute!" She leans over and rolls my jeans and then stands up, clapping again. "You actually look cute!"

I sniff, flattening the shirt. I try not to smile, but Brooke looks so goofy, doing her little dance in the stinky middle school bathroom, that I can't help it.

She hands me her limp backpack after taking out her flowery make-up bag. "Here. I know how weird you are about being unprepared and stuff. Please don't carry it around all day. Backpacks are for lockers. You'll look like such a sixth-grader with that thing."

"I am a sixth-grader."

"Exactly."

And even though she's kind of making fun of me, I can't believe Brooke would give me her only backpack on the first day of school.

"Thanks," I say.

"Oh, shut up." She swings the door open to an empty hallway. "Let's go."

# nine

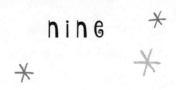

HOMEROOM IS ALREADY OVER, so I go straight to Independent Study, for the smart kids who belong in fancy private schools. Except my schedule just says "Independent Study, Room 235."

Brooke takes me to the right stairway. "Don't get anything on those jeans or —"

"I know." I wipe my nose. Still clean.

"Or that shirt, okay? They're like my —"

"I know!" I wave goodbye and push into the flow of kids moving up the stairs. I already missed my first homeroom; there's no way I'm going to be late to Independent Study.

When I walk into Room 235, there are a few kids I don't recognize looking for seats. And then I spot Katherine-with-a-K Babcock bouncing in the rolling chair at the computer. Katherine-with-a-K is the entire reason I did not win the science fair last year, after she accidentally butt-bumped my fruit flies from their glass display onto the tile floor. There were fruit flies in the school for the entire rest of the year.

This year I will keep my project as far from Katherine-with-a-K as possible. And I'll win, because without Elizabeth here, I am probably the only real scientist left in our grade.

"Hey, Madeline!" Katherine says too loud. "This is so cool, right? Being in Independent Study together?"

The teacher sticks her head out from the supply closet. "Go ahead and find your seats. I'll be right with you!"

I ignore Katherine-with-a-K and toss Brooke's backpack onto the two-person table directly in front of the teacher's desk before any of the other kids can claim it. I'm inspecting the contents (now just three gum wrappers and a nail file) when Amy Taylor walks in. Her backpack is the size of a small refrigerator. She teeters in the doorway under the weight of it until Katherine-with-a-K jumps up and yanks her into the room.

"Thanks," Amy says, straightening her headband.

"What in the world do you have in there?" I say.

She circles around and sets her backpack on my table, squirming like an upside-down bug until she's able to slide her arms out. "Encyclopedias."

"E-N-C-Y-C-L-O-P-E-D-I-A," Katherine-with-a-K sings at full volume. She's the district spelling bee champ, five years running.

"The library is giving them away, since they got a new set," Amy says.

"What are you researching?" I say.

She shakes her head. "Just reading."

My dad and I do our research in journals where scientists publish the conclusions to their laboratory research. Like the time we learned tofu can stunt your growth. A fact my mom did not appreciate.

Our teacher appears out of the closet and writes her name on the board: Mrs. Blickman. Timothy Tangier is right on her heels, showing her a T. rex 3D puzzle that I recognize from the gift shop at the science museum. I wonder if he gets a 10 percent discount like Elizabeth and I do for being such loyal members.

I'm wishing I had my lab notebook so I could write an SOP on *How to Properly Introduce Yourself to a Teacher* when the girl who almost stole Grandpa's retirement clock at the estate sale waltzes in. What is she doing here? Does this look like a class for criminals?

She puts her backpack on the table right next to mine and waves like I'm her best-best friend, her bracelets jingle-jangling. "Do you remember me? Riley? From the estate sale yesterday? I'm going to be an astronaut, remember?"

And then I write an SOP in my head on *How to Avoid an Unwanted Conversation.*

*Step 1. Appear very confused. Like you've just stepped off an airplane and your ears are super plugged.*

I let her babble on about the estate sale.

*Step 2. Squint and shake your head yes and no at the same time.*

"You remember?" she says, brightening. "Yes? No?"

And then I just sit down because I'm confusing myself and getting strange looks from other students. Amy Taylor is paging through her *C* encyclopedia and saying something to me about coyotes, but I ignore her. Can't a girl just sit in annoyed silence because she's having a bad day?

Amy and Riley talk over my head about coyotes and carp and cholera like I'm not even here. Which is fine by me, because who feels like talking when they're sandwiched between a maniac encyclopedia kid and a known almost-thief? I bet Riley doesn't even return her library books on time.

Finally Mrs. Blickman gets class started. "Welcome to Independent Study, a place for independent thinkers and adventure seekers! This class is a place to explore, research, learn! There is only one project. One grade. One assignment." She sits on her desk and stares at us, a finger raised. "Think of something you've always wanted to do" — Timothy Tangier raises his hand but she shakes her head at him — "and do it."

If Elizabeth were here, we'd be sitting at this little table together, sharing pencils and exchanging erasers. She'd be horrified along with me that I have to carry around Brooke's nearly empty backpack, and we'd worry about my own well-stocked backpack just sitting unsupervised on an empty bus. Instead, I'm here with a girl who's pulling encyclopedias out of her backpack one at a time and isn't even paying attention.

"Can I go to the National Spelling Bee as my project?" Katherine-with-a-K blurts.

"Well, this class can't get you into the National Spelling Bee, but you could most certainly try to qualify and write about the experience," Mrs. Blickman says.

"T-R-E-M-E-N-D-O-U-S!" Katherine says, and I miss Elizabeth again because nobody even giggles or flinches at her outburst. In fact, there's a chance Amy is sleeping with her eyes open, because who could read about jackals for ten minutes?

"After completing the project, you'll write a term paper about it. I'll pass out the detailed outline later this week. Until then, think about your topic and get started!" Mrs. Blickman stands up and stretches. "Jot down some ideas. Talk with your neighbor. Make some friends."

I stare at the blank table in front of me. No paper. No pencil. What's the point of a backpack with no school supplies? Brooke's right; it's like we're not even related. Amy's tower of books is creeping into my space and I push it away, trying not to knock the entire stack over. It's going to be a long year with Katherine-with-a-K, Timothy, and Amy E-N-C-Y-C-L-O-P-E-D-I-A. Not to mention the thief, who is now staring at me. I wipe my nose. Clean.

"Need some paper?" Riley says. "I always come to class prepared."

"No thanks."

"A pen?" She rummages in her bag and pulls out something that looks exactly like the official Space Camp pen I've seen online.

"Is that—"

"Yep." She nods. "From Space Camp. I'll probably interview an astronaut for my project since I know a whole bunch now."

And then she raises her hand and announces her astronaut project to the entire class—and says that she's going to be a scientist. Mrs. Blickman says how wonderful that is, but I can barely hear her over my coughing fit.

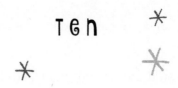

# TEN

I WAIT FOR school to be over. Wait to be reunited with my backpack, which finally ended up in the school office. Wait until my first day at this horrible place called middle school ends. On the bus home I swab a window and then lean down to get a sample from the floor. I don't even care that the kid across the aisle looks at me like I just licked the seat. I carefully stow my swabs and hug my backpack for the rest of the ride.

When I get home, I say a quick hi to Mom, who's on the phone with Nana. I try to grab a snack from the pantry and head back out the door, but Mom hands me the phone.

"Hi, Nana," I say, setting my backpack down. Her dog, Mouse, is barking in the background.

"Hi, sweetie!" she says like we haven't talked in a million years. "Do you feel different now that you're a big-time middle-schooler?"

"Kind of," I say. Except I don't mean that in a good way.

"Wish I could be there in person to hear all about it. You're not too old for a hug from your old Nana, right?"

"You're not old, Nana," I say.

"You sound tired. Is everything okay? Do I need to come down there with a bag of candy?"

"I'm fine, Nana."

"I can be there in an hour flat," she says, Mouse still yipping. "Because kids need candy too, you know. Tell your mom it can't be all kale and green stuff all the time."

"I'll tell her," I say, looking at Mom and smiling.

"Alllll right." Mom's pulling the phone away. "Say goodbye."

We hang up with Nana and I take a granola bar out of the closet and grab my backpack.

"Going to the library?" Mom asks. It's what Elizabeth and I do after school every day.

"Yep." I head back out the door. It's a lie. Elizabeth already told me she has to stay after school today for club sign-ups. One day an aspiring famous scientist, the next a cold-hearted middle school lying machine.

The university quad is quiet and green. My feet sink into the lush grass and it feels so much like summer, I get a lump in my throat. The door to the science building where my dad works is propped open and I walk into the sunny atrium. Sometimes when Dad's still giving a lecture and I have to wait, I pretend to be a college kid, sitting in the puffy chair by the trickling fountain. But now there's a girl with black-rimmed glasses sitting there, typing on her laptop.

The building is a research hospital: half laboratories, half hospital, with real, live patients and sickness. Bench-top to bedside, Grandpa called it. I type 0515, the access code I know by heart, on the keypad by the door that leads to the labs. The door buzzes open and I veer left into the biochemistry wing, where rooms are crowded with people in lab coats. Twisted glass tubes and giant instruments cover black benchtops. It's hot and smells like cleaner. I dodge red biohazard bags and giant bottles waiting to be picked up by the facility guys.

When I reach Dad's lab, I check the autoclave room first, leaning in through the doorway, but all I hear is the deep rumbling snore of the machine. The giant silver sterilizer is embedded in the wall, its huge door locked closed with metal teeth like an ancient bank vault. I've seen pictures of what an autoclave can do if the blistering steam builds up behind the door: one error on the pressure gauge, and BOOM!

"Maddie?"

I slam the door.

"What are you doing here?" Dad says. "I thought you'd be at the library with Elizabeth."

A thousand pictures of today flash through my mind. Astronauts, encyclopedias, empty backpacks, blood. I can't find a word for a single one. "I just —"

"Did something happen?"

I nod. "Nosebleed."

Dad looks like he needs a chair all of a sudden. "When? Does Mom know?"

When Brooke has a nosebleed, there's always drama. I just want nothing. "A girl in my class went to Space Camp this summer," I say.

"Maddie, did you go see the nurse?"

A high-pitched alarm has just started from the auto-clave.

"She even had an official pen."

Dad grabs my elbow. "We've talked about this. It's no joke. If you have any kind of bleeding at all you go to the nurse, and she'll call Mom or me."

"It barely lasted five minutes."

"This is what we're going to do." He swings on his lab coat, then hands me a pair of goggles and a visitor lab coat. It's about ten sizes too big and stained with rust on the sleeve, but science is not a fashion statement. I push my goggles all the way up on my nose and trail Dad into the autoclave room. "We'll deal with the autoclave, but then it's straight to Phlebotomy."

Where they take blood samples. More blood.

"Any dizziness?" he says. "Fainting? Have you been eating?"

The alarm is deafening. But real scientists don't cover their ears like babies. Dad punches the big red button by the read-out screen and the room is silent again.

"No, Dad, just a nosebleed." My ears ring.

Dad yanks on the wheel to open the autoclave door, but it doesn't budge. "I've been waiting all morning for this glassware." His cheeks are pink from the effort.

It's been the same story for four years. So much of his research depends on this uncooperative beast. Dad pulls once more on the wheel, but the autoclave's not ready to open his mouth. Dad taps on the pressure gauges and then lets me try. I pat the big steel belly and give a gentle tug. One of these days I'm going to get it.

"Maybe he needs a little more time," I say.

Dad tosses his goggles onto a lab table. "Ten minutes, autoclave," he says. "Ten more minutes or I'm calling service and prying you open."

"I don't want to give blood, Dad," I say. But he's already holding the door open.

"Just a small sample."

This is what happens when you have a bleeding disorder and your dad is a research hematologist. I follow him, dragging my feet. "Dad, I came here to talk to you about something else. I need a job or something."

Dad laughs a little. "Planning on running away?"

"We have a project at school and I need a great topic. I want to work in a real lab, like a real scientist. Make discoveries."

Dad looks at me. "They don't like kids working in the lab, Maddie."

I'm offended. "I'm hardly a regular kid, Dad."

He ignores me, and when we get to Phlebotomy, everyone is busy working. Which means taking people's blood for tests. I was never grossed out by this before, but somehow I don't feel that great today. I sit in a plastic chair, hoping nobody has time to draw my blood.

Dad's lab assistant, Tyrone, walks by in the hall, a mug of coffee in his hand. He skids to a stop. It's always Brooke sitting in Phlebotomy with Dad, not me.

"Just a little nosebleed," I say. It's not like I have Von Willebrand as bad as Brooke, right? I change the subject. "Dad won't let me work in the lab for a school project," I tell Tyrone. "I'm going to get an F."

Dad throws his hands up and Tyrone laughs. "I could use a glassware cleaner," he says.

"I'm not going to be a dishwasher."

Tyrone is basically a kid himself, just out of college. And he runs entire experiments by himself even though he gets written up about five times a month for wearing flip-flops in the lab. Which is something I'd never do, as it's clearly forbidden in Step 3a of the *Personal Protection SOP* hanging on the front door of the lab.

"The thing is," I continue, "there's this new girl who thinks she's the next super-famous scientist, and she's going to interview an astronaut." They stare at me. "A real one."

Dad shakes his head. "I don't think the department heads would like it."

"Actually, doesn't Molecular Biology have a high school intern?" Tyrone says. "And also Microbiology. Maddie's not *that* much younger."

I brighten, sitting up in my seat. "Just a small project? Like maybe I could decode the genome of a flea or something? Or put some of the stuff that grows on my petri dishes under a microscope so I can identify it?" Without a microscope, it's pretty hard to figure out exactly what kind of man-eating bacteria or fungus is actually on my petri plate. Staphylococcus, E. coli, Candida albicans. They all look pretty much the same.

"She could inventory the freezer," Tyrone says.

"That was your job three months ago, Tyrone." Dad takes a giant breath. "We'll see. Let's talk to Mom about it. If it's for a school project, then maybe."

I straighten. "Really?" Tyrone gives me a double high-five and I sit back in my seat.

Janice from Phlebotomy is rushing over now, her tray of blood stuff balanced on one hand. "I'm not so happy to see you here," she says, pushing up my sleeve.

I close my eyes as she ties something rubber around my arm, pushing on my veins. All of a sudden I'm sweating like it's ninety degrees in here. I write an SOP real-quick in my head on *How to Survive a Needle.*

*Step 1. Close your eyes tight.*

*Step 2. Pretend you're safe at the library in the middle of the science stacks, reading* — OUCH!

"Sorry," Janice says, rubbing my other arm. "Almost over."

But I know it's not. They're always taking Brooke's blood. Running tests, checking levels. I look at Dad, but he's already prepping a tray for my tests, clinking glass tubes into a rack, handing it to another phlebotomist with instructions I don't understand. Janice is holding my hand, just barely, and I pretend she's Grandpa. Because that's what he would have done. He'd have held my hands, even if I didn't want it, even if Janice kept yelling at him to get out of the way.

"Only thirty or so milliliters, Maddie. Your body won't even notice," Dad says, all science.

We're finished, and I stand up like it was no big deal, but my legs feel heavy and my eyes are watery. Tyrone pats me on the back, nearly pushing me over. "Good job."

"Now, don't come back, you hear me?" Janice jokes.

Dad checks his watch and I follow him into the break room across from Phlebotomy. I ate here so many times with Dad over the summer. I didn't even mind all the needles and blood right across the hall because it was all part of being a scientist.

But now I sit with my back to the door, Dad sloshing a mug of hot chocolate onto the table in front of me. He wipes up the dribbles, clumsy, making them worse. When he leans over to dab them up, he spills more. We are a disaster.

"Is there much stuff left at Grandpa's house?" I ask when Dad sits with me at the table.

"Not too much."

"I can help if you want."

Dad snorts, because mostly my helping has meant

me trying to smuggle more stuff back to our house. "No thanks. You worry about school and I'll worry about the house."

His pager goes off; one of the autoclave's alarms is ringing. I'm used to this, since our lunches are interrupted 80 percent of the time by one scientific crisis or another. We put our mugs in the sink and Dad kisses me on the forehead.

"Aloha," he says, which means both hello and goodbye in Hawaii. That is the first place we're going after Dad gets all the results from his super-important experiment. Our first vacation in years and years. And as he steers me out the door, I think about how very much I need one.

# ELEVEN

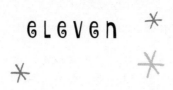

THE NEXT DAY after school, I head right to the college library. I peek through the little circle window in the door to the art history stacks and see that Elizabeth is already perched on her usual stool, hunched over her books. There's a baggie of jelly beans next to her, and a pile of green ones she set aside for me. I feel a burst of happiness that everything is the same in our little corner of the library. I push open the door and throw my backpack onto the table next to her.

"Jasper Johns Middle School, where students reach their potential," Elizabeth reads, looking at the booklet I'm pulling out.

"I have to read the student handbook and sign the page in the back. They call that homework." I collapse into a chair. "You have no idea what regular middle school is like."

"You're lucky," Elizabeth says, her braided hair shiny in the fluorescent lighting. "I have a five-hundred-word essay on biomes due tomorrow, just the third day of school."

She's wearing her new school uniform, a white collared shirt with a green cardigan sweater and a khaki pleated skirt. "I also have a lab safety quiz tomorrow."

"You have labs?" I say. "What kind of labs?"

She looks at me. "Nothing huge. The normal kinds of labs, like chemistry, biology, and physics. They even have their own autoclave. Just a little one that sits on a desk, but . . ."

"Does it work?" I say. Our school doesn't have one lab. Not even one.

"It's not the same without you," Elizabeth says. "Really. You don't need labs, anyway. How many kids grow up with someone like your dad?"

I don't feel like talking anymore. I push my student handbook aside and take out Grandpa's lab notebook, trying to remember all the SOPs I thought of yesterday at school when my notebook was stuck in my backpack on the bus, unattended.

"Not like it's that great anyway. I mean, they have lab glasses from the 1950s. That can't be sanitary, right?" Elizabeth laughs too loud and then quickly buries herself in her book again. *Exploring the Tundra*. She pushes my pile of jelly beans closer to me and I bite one in half, the sourness making my mouth pucker.

"Is that all of your homework?" Elizabeth asks, her voice upbeat, like she's trying to change the subject.

It's why we always meet in the university library, every day at four o'clock, post after-school snacks: to do homework. Way back in the art history stacks, with their puke-green linoleum floors, we can get our work done and eat jelly beans without being seen by the librarian.

"Pretty much. I have to write an essay about my summer, but it's not due until next week." I erase what I've written so far on *How to Protect Your Eardrums from Katherine-with-a-K* and start a new SOP: *How to Go to Public Middle School Without Your Best Friend.* I cover the title, because it's not like Elizabeth is having the same problem.

"Do you have someone to sit with at lunch?" I say.

"Yep." She puts her book down. "There's this really nice girl I met at orientation before the school year started. She sits next to me in math. You'd love her."

I frown. "Does she bring you hummus and collect pencils and belong to the science museum?"

Elizabeth reaches for another book. "Stop. You'll always be my best friend."

"Pretty much my only lunchroom options are

Katherine-with-a-K, some new girl who thinks she's a genius scientist, Amy Taylor, and Timothy Tangier."

"Amy's pretty nice, isn't she? You should sit with them."

I cross my arms. Yesterday and today I didn't want to sit with anyone, so I sat in the bathroom until the bell rang and sneaked a granola bar on my way to science.

Elizabeth slides over some more green jelly beans. "If you ignore Timothy and his boring dinosaur talk and Katherine spelling everything all the time, they're not so bad."

"What?" I can't believe she's saying this. "They're so loud all the time, and everyone's always looking at them, and they even chew with their mouths open —"

"Sometimes you chew with your mouth open," Elizabeth says. "And you're not always the easiest to get along with, either."

"Hey!" I drop a jelly bean and it skitters across the floor. "What does that mean?"

Elizabeth closes her book. "Well, you can be pushy sometimes, and you always want things your way."

I chase my jelly bean down and toss it toward the trash can. It pings off the side and rolls across the floor again. "So do you!" I point my finger. "It's just not the same this year. They're not like us."

"I know," Elizabeth says. "Just keep an open mind, okay?"

She sounds like my mom, but I don't say anything more. Instead I pretend to be super focused on writing my essay while Elizabeth takes notes from her tundra book.

It's barely a minute later when Elizabeth hops up, looking at her watch. "I have to go." She stuffs her books back into her bag. "I have a study group tonight."

"Oh." I stand up too. "Okay."

She pulls her green cardigan tighter around her and hefts her backpack on. "It's a night-sky project, and we have to use my telescope."

"Cool. I have a really hard project in Independent Study, too."

"Bye!" Elizabeth rushes out, and I don't even get to tell her about my nosebleed. It's fine that she left, though, because there's nothing worse than watching your friend do a bunch of homework that requires real brain power while you pretend to write a boring essay.

# TWELVE

I TAKE THE LONG way home through the university soccer fields so I don't have to pass Grandpa's house. I wonder if his duck lamp is still on his desk, or if the stack of playing cards is still on the coffee table next to the SOP for *How to Play Go-Fish*. Sometimes I'd add a few lines, like the winner always gets a piece of candy as a trophy. And if Grandpa's mind was as jumbled as Dad said it had become, then why did he always let me win, and how did he remember to have my favorite butterscotch candies tucked into his desk drawer?

"Heads up!" someone yells from the field, and I turn to see a soccer ball arcing toward me. It smacks me on the side of the head and I trip over my own feet, landing face-first in the AstroTurf. When I lift myself up, there is blood on my hands, on the green grass that's not real grass, and on my shirt.

No. Not again. Not so soon.

And then I'm surrounded by a sweaty, muddy group

of heavy-breathing middle school soccer players, talking to me all at once. One guy takes his shirt off and stuffs it under my nose, and I hold my breath because I hate the smell of sweat and boys. I try to give it back.

"I don't want to ruin your shirt," I say. There are numbers on it, and a name that I recognize. When I look up, Brooke's own Dexter Sully frowns down at me.

"We tried to warn you, but you were in your own world," he says, pushing the shirt onto my nose again. "You okay?"

I nod, but really I'm not sure. I need ice, and maybe someone to call my mom.

"You aiming for her, Sully?" An old guy comes around the corner. His shorts are too tight and the whistle around his neck swings with every step. "Can we get some ice over here?" he calls toward the bleachers, then pushes through the group and leans over me. "Don't tell me she's crying!" he yells.

And I don't know if he's yelling at me or if he just yells all the time, but I start crying harder. Like an elementary school baby who doesn't know any real-life astronauts.

Coach leans in and pulls my hand away from my nose. "Not broken," he confirms. "Sully, fix this. The rest of you pansies, back out on the field!"

Dexter puts on his sweatshirt and keeps sitting with

me even after the ice comes. It's been six minutes, and panic is tingling up my legs. What if it doesn't stop this time?

Coach is back. "Where do you live?" he asks, pointing his whistle at me.

I motion toward the tennis courts. "Fountain Drive."

He smacks Dexter on the arm. "You broke her nose, you walk her home."

"It's not broken," we say at the same time.

"Sure is a lot of blood," Coach says, lingering for a moment before he takes off to yell at a player tying his shoes on the sideline.

I stand up. "I can walk myself. I'm almost twelve." The shirt isn't keeping up with my nosebleed anymore. Nine minutes. Already longer than my first one.

Dexter stands up. "You can't walk home now. You're still bleeding."

There's no SOP that says you have to sit down and wait for a nosebleed to stop. I can practically see our neighbor's roof in the distance. I walk off toward the tennis courts and Dexter trips after me in his cleats, saying, "Seriously. You should sit down."

By the time I'm on our street, the blood has stopped. When I look down at myself, I cringe, because it looks like I've just barely survived the zombie apocalypse. Mr. Sid, reading a book on his front porch, nearly chokes when he sees me.

"Just a nosebleed," I say, waving.

Dexter waves too. "Accidentally hit her with a soccer ball."

Mr. Sid looks like he wants to say a million things, but then Bark comes trotting down the street, off-leash, tongue hanging out of his mouth. Mr. Sid jumps into action, grabbing his garden hose, acting like we're not even here.

"Thanks for walking me home," I say, unlocking my front door.

"Next time someone yells 'heads up,' duck, okay?"

I promise, and he leaves just as Brooke sees me coming in. "Another nosebleed?" And then she spots Dexter walking away. "Are you kidding me? Dexter Sully just walked you home?" She grabs his shirt from me, stained with more red splotches than mud and grass, and runs toward the kitchen. "You have his shirt? We have to put it in water! We can save this, can't we?"

"It's just a T-shirt with his name on it, Brooke," I say. "He wouldn't give his actual soccer jersey to a lowly sixth-grader." Especially the idiot kind who walks into soccer balls.

"Madeline?" Mom calls.

I backpedal and run up the stairs before Mom or Dad can see me. I peel my ruined clothes off and stand in a hot shower, letting all the blood, sweat, and tears — literally — go down the drain with the soapy water.

# Thirteen

WHEN I COME back downstairs, I'm carrying a pitcher, some empty petri dishes, and my lab notebook. Time to make more agar. Without a layer of agar on the bottom of the petri dishes, the bacteria won't grow. I used my last two prepared dishes for my school bus swabs, which, surprisingly, aren't growing anything on them yet.

Dad is teetering on the arm of our big chair, leveling the naked lady over the fireplace. Mom eyes me when I join her in the kitchen. "Be quick, I'm starting dinner," she says.

"I'll be super fast." I pull out the big pot, some beef stock powder, a little bit of sugar, and some gelatin from the cupboards. I slosh some water into the pot and start it boiling.

Mom squeezes my shoulders. "I saw the shirt; I know you had another nosebleed. I made an appointment with the doctor for tomorrow, okay?"

"It wasn't the same. A soccer ball hit me." But I figured this was coming. I've never had to go before, but Brooke goes to a special doctor for bleeding disorders once a year, sometimes more when she bleeds a lot.

"Can I go to Derek McLaughlin's birthday party this weekend?" Brooke asks from the couch.

Mom grabs my face, inspecting it. "Show me where the ball hit you."

"I'm fine." I try to change the subject. "Mom, Elizabeth's school has three labs. They get to do real lab stuff. There's even a little autoclave, Dad. Jasper Johns has nothing like that." The stove is fizz-popping from the water I spilled on the burner.

Dad freezes, still perched on the chair. "Does it work?"

Mom's walking away from me. "You haven't given school a chance yet, Maddie."

"We don't even have a library!" I say. Mom stops, because she knows that besides agar plates, autoclaves, and science collections, libraries are required for my health and well-being.

"There's a library," Brooke says. "It's just being remodeled."

"Forever!" I say, dumping all my ingredients into the boiling water. Mom puts her hands on her hips. I hate when she stands that way, like a mean stone statue. I cross my arms. "You can see that painting from the door, you know." I turn to the stove, breathing in the warm soup smell, and give my agar a stir. My hair, still wet from my shower, drips cool water down my back.

"Hello?" Brooke knocks on the wall. "Earth to my parents. Can I go or not?"

"Isn't Derek McLaughlin in high school?" I say. "The kid who just got out of juvie?"

"Shut up, Maddie!" Brooke's face is red. If she's not careful, she'll give herself a nosebleed.

I shut off the stove and leave my concoction to cool, then see an envelope for Dad on top of today's mail. It's from the science center.

"A high school party?" Dad steps off the arm of the chair for a better look at his leveling job.

"Wait. As in juvenile hall?" Mom says.

I grab the letter off the pile and hold it up to the light. New membership cards? I shake the envelope.

"I don't like the sound of this party, Brooke," Mom says, looking at her painting. "I'll have to talk to his parents."

"You're not calling his parents!" Brooke's standing now.

"It's quite a painting, dear," Dad says, staring at the lady on the wall. "Do you think over the fireplace is the best spot for it?"

"Daniel." Mom's back in the kitchen with me now, pulling out tofu and basil and olive oil. "The fireplace is the focal point of the whole house. Where else would it belong?"

"At the dump," Brooke says in a half whisper.

"I heard that, young lady." Mom pauses, her spatula in the air. "You just be happy you have a mother so in tune with art these days."

"Can I open this?" I show Dad the letter, but he grabs it from me and holds it to his chest.

"Nope." He's grinning.

"What do you even know about juvenile hall, Maddie?" Brooke says, collapsing onto one of the stools at the kitchen counter. "And for your information, it was all a big misunderstanding. He didn't vandalize the police car — it was his friend Rocky."

"Dad. What's it for?" I pull at a corner of the letter and it slides out of his grip.

"I'm pretty sure you're not going to this party," Mom says.

"Why do you let her do these disgusting experiments? She's stinking up the entire house!" Brooke snatches the letter out of my hands.

"Hey!"

"Everyone stop." Dad takes the envelope from Brooke. He looks at Mom. "Should we let her open it early?"

Brooke plugs her nose. "You better not get her a phone."

"I knew it was for me!" I'm hopping with excitement now.

"If you open it now, it won't be a surprise on your birthday," Mom warns.

"I didn't get a phone until I was thirteen," Brooke grumbles.

It could be anything. A gift card so I can buy a microscope? A private birthday tour of the telescope exhibit? A secret behind-the-scenes look at the planetarium?

Dad hands me the envelope. "You decide when you want to open it."

I rip it open so fast, the contents of the letter flutter to the floor. And then I can't believe what I'm seeing. Three tickets to the sold-out Snoozatarium. Three. On my birthday.

"How —" My voice cracks. "Are these for real?"

"We thought Dad could take you and Elizabeth," Mom says from near the stovetop. "Like a small birthday party."

"Smallest birthday party in the world." Brooke snorts and climbs off the stool.

"Actually, I have a ton of friends, thank you very much."

"Ha!" She lingers at the top of the stairs down to the basement. "Actually, you don't, but whatever." She stomps down to her room.

"That's not really a bedroom, Brooke!" Mom calls. "Daniel, I don't like her sleeping down there. Should we make her move back upstairs?"

Dad is kind of laughing at me because I'm still just staring at the tickets like I half expect them to disappear in a puff of smoke. "What do you think, Maddie?"

"I can't wait to tell Elizabeth!" I say, kissing Dad on the cheek. "How did you get these? You know it's sold out!"

"The university had some tickets on hold for employees, so I jumped on them."

Elizabeth is going to freak out. All summer we took turns checking to see if we'd moved up on the wait list, but we never did. Nobody is giving up their Snoozatarium tickets.

My agar is cooling fast, so I hang the tickets high on the refrigerator door and line up my petri dishes. One by one, I lift each lid and pour a layer of warm, soupy agar into the bottom. I tap the plates to get all the bubbles out. Later tonight, when they look like solid Jell-O, I'll stack them up and take them to my room.

When I turn around, Mom looks serious.

"What?"

"I don't like this idea of working in the lab, Maddie," Mom says. "Dad told me."

"It's for school, though," I say. "A really important school project."

"It would just be a small job, Evelyn." Dad inspects my petri dishes, tapping one against the counter to get out more bubbles.

"But not too small?" I ask.

"Tyrone is right," Dad says. "She's not a little girl anymore, and it would be great for her to get some early lab experience. If she still wants to be a scientist."

"Yes! Yes, I do!" I say, bouncing. I could have a job. In a real science lab. I might kiss that Tyrone when I see him.

"What about the chemicals?" Mom says, her tofu sticking to the pan now. "Didn't Tyrone explode something recently?"

"Minor," Dad says. "Barely even an explosion."

"Oh, please, Mom! Please, please, please!"

Mom swats at me with her spatula and I don't even care when a piece of barf-tofu gets flung onto my shirt. "Do you have goggles for her?"

Dad turns the burner down, our dinner crackling and burning. "Yes, of course."

"Real goggles?" I say.

"We can always order a pair in the right size," Dad says. "It's fine, Evelyn. A few departments have high school interns. Maddie will be fine."

Mom groans and looks at me, folding her arms. "You keep away from Tyrone and his explosions. And always wear your goggles and gloves and lab coat and whatever else they have."

And I do a leap like I used to do in ballet because, finally, my day of suffering is looking like the greatest day in all my life. First, tickets to the Snoozatarium, and now a job in a lab? I collapse onto the floor, but nobody rushes over because they know I've collapsed from happiness.

When we sit down to our dinner of partially scorched tofu balls and noodles, I open my lab notebook and write an SOP on *How to Make Friends with an Autoclave*.

*Step 1. Always check his temperatures to make sure they're perfectly right.*

*Step 2. Never slam his doors or* —

"No notebooks at the table, Madeline," Dad says.

Brooke burps at me from across the table, but I don't care. Because starting tomorrow I'm going to be a real-life scientist working in a real-life lab.

In your face, Astronaut Girl!

# fourteen

GOING TO THE DOCTOR actually means an entire day off from school because we have to drive all the way to the hemophilia treatment center. The doctor tells me to be gentle with my nose while it heals from the soccer ball incident and gives me a nose spray in case of a bleeding episode. By the time we get home, school's nearly over.

Mom insists I take the rest of the day as a mental health day, which in fact almost gives me hives, and help her get a jump on her organic dryer ball orders for Pumpkin Fest. She already has fourteen orders, six more than last year, now that the news is spreading that her eco-friendly balls fluff and soften towels just as well as dryer sheets, but without all the chemicals.

We wind wool into balls on our front porch and watch Mr. Sid work in his garden. Each time Bark the beast makes an appearance, Mr. Sid is ready, but unfortunately

Bark isn't fazed by the balled-up newspaper Mr. Sid lobs over the fence. In fact, after he sees to his business, Bark collects a few balls of newspaper in his mouth and trots back home like they're a gift.

At four o'clock Mom lets me take a break from the dryer balls, so I pull the Snoozatarium tickets off the fridge and run to the library to show Elizabeth, my entire body tingling with excitement. We probably won't do any homework today because we'll just talk about the sleepover the whole time. What might be in the astronaut breakfast. What we'll do if we have to sleep next to the mummified chicken from ancient Chile.

When I get to our spot in the art history section, the room is dim even though Elizabeth is almost always here first. I swing into the room and the lights brighten. I tuck the tickets safely into my backpack, then take out my lab notebook and make a list while I wait.

*What to Pack for a Snoozatarium*

*1. Sleeping bag, preferably science-themed.*

*2. Flashlight for bathroom breaks.*

*3. Lab gloves in case someone hands you a rare and dangerous specimen.*

*4. Jelly beans.*

*5. A science dictionary.*

*6. Earplugs in case they don't turn off the
   humpback whale exhibit.*

I look out through the little round window in the door. No Elizabeth. It's after 4:30. I add more to my list.

*7. A protein bar, because the astronaut breakfast
   might be freeze-dried fish cakes.*

*8. Goggles, obviously.*

I'm running out of ideas. Did Elizabeth forget? I wait awhile longer, and then I finally pack my things and double-check that the tickets are still safe in the front zippered pocket.

When I get home I call Elizabeth right away, but her mother tells me, "I'm sorry, Madeline, Elizabeth has a lot of homework tonight. She can't play after school like she used to."

"You mean do homework together?" I'm on the kitchen phone and Brooke is painting her nails at the counter. I turn my back to her.

"Right, right. Elizabeth said you don't have as much homework as she does this year, so maybe that's not going to work out."

"She can't go to the library anymore?" My face feels hot.

"She needs to focus. But you know, she can probably take it a little easier on Fridays. How about she sees you at the library then?"

"Oh. Okay." I really need to tell Elizabeth about the tickets. I've been holding this news for a whole day. "Can I talk to her for just a second?"

"Not tonight, sweetheart."

I hang up and Brooke is right there. "Best friend problems? You know I'm an expert on that sort of thing." But I can't tell if she's being mean or for-real, so I brush past her and go up to my room.

I write down all the SOPs I can remember from Grandpa. *How to Tell a Joke. How to Apologize. How to Say Thank You. How to Transform your Cupcake into an Icing Sandwich.* I record them all in my notebook. And then I write one for myself.

> *How to Tell if Your Best Friend Is Still Your Best Friend.*
>
> *Step 1. If she tells you that you're hard to get along with and pushy and stubborn, that's not a good sign.*

Step 2. If she ditches you at the library even though you go to the library after school together every single day, that is also not a good sign.

Step 3. If you get another bad sign the next time you see her, then maybe your best friend isn't your best friend anymore.

# fifteen

THE NEXT DAY at lunch, I see Katherine-with-a-K sitting at a table with Riley the Thief and I creep away in the other direction. There *has* to be another seat somewhere in this crowded place; I can't stay in the bathroom again. Katherine spots me and spells "G-U-T-E-N T-A-G!" in a shouty voice, adding, "That means 'good day' in German!" I ignore her, but she stands up, waving. "Madeline! Over here!"

It feels like the entire lunchroom stops to look at me. Elizabeth would never do something like this.

I quickly make my way over to Katherine-with-a-K's table so she'll stop spell-shouting at me, while I desperately look for an alternative. But all the tables are taken by hordes of sixth-graders, greasy with tater tots and grilled cheese.

And then I see an opening at a table by the trash cans. One glorious empty seat. But when I get close, I see that the seat has already been taken by a giant unsanitary glob of gum. My first instinct is to whip out a swab and get a good sample, but there are too many witnesses. Instead, I peek back over my shoulder.

Katherine-with-a-K is still standing, watching me. There's no other option. I go back.

Amy stands next to the table holding her I'D RATHER BE READING lunch bag. "I'm going to the library," she declares. "The construction has to be nearly done by now. They've got to let me in." She turns and heads for the door, Timothy Tangier clambering after her. Even though Amy has a weird obsession with encyclopedias and Timothy with dinosaurs, I have to respect their perseverance.

I sit down, and Katherine, who has hardly stopped talking, sits down too. "I could use a chocolate milk," she says. "C-H-O-C-O-L-A-T-E!"

She launches herself into the lunch line and I open my bag, trying to ignore Riley the Thief, who is basically staring at me. She's wearing a braggy necklace that I saw on the Space Camp website; it practically screams "I went to Space Camp! I went to Space Camp!" It's an astronaut reaching for a star that's really a fake diamond.

Riley dabs her mouth with a napkin and touches her necklace. "I got this at camp," she says. "I saved my allowance for three months ahead of time. Want to try it on?"

I shake my head and wonder how many times I'd have

to take the trash out to pay my way to Space Camp. Probably one million-katrillion times.

Katherine-with-a-K isn't even back with her C-H-O-C-O-L-A-T-E milk when a red-faced Amy falls into a seat at our table, her seventy-pound bag thudding to the concrete floor beside her. Timothy Tangier sits next to me. "Still no library," he says, cleaning his glasses with his sleeve.

"Everybody has to stay in the cafeteria at lunch," Amy says. "With all these people." She looks at the kids talking and laughing and carrying trays full of pasta and milk and ice cream cups. If one kid tripped over Amy's backpack, it would cause a thirty-kid pile-up. And then Katherine-with-a-K is back, shaking up her chocolate milk and offering a sip to everyone at the table.

Amy unpacks her *C* encyclopedia and flips it open to a close-up of a cockroach, all antennae and buggy eyes, which makes us both jump. Timothy Tangier cranes his neck to see what she's reading, the smell of the hard-boiled egg in his hand making me want to puke. I'm pretty sure I've seen a cockroach or two in our basement. Is Brooke really so sick of me that she'd rather sleep with a bunch of cockroaches than in the same room as her own sister? Am I really that hard to get along with?

"Hey, does it say in there that cockroaches like to eat birdseed?" I ask, because there are like three giant bags of birdseed sitting in Brooke's basement bedroom-that's-not-a-bedroom.

Amy looks up. "Cockroaches are omnivores. They eat everything. They'll eat a shoe if you give it to them." Then she flips to the page on Colorado.

"Attention, please!" Riley stands up. "We're having a tea party at my house, and I'd love if you guys could make it." She places a pile of flyers, glittery and smelling like perfume, on the table. Her bracelets clink and slide down her arm. "It's a cupcake tasting for my mom's new bakery. She's the best baker in town, you know."

"I would L-O-V-E to!" Katherine-with-a-K shouts.

"The first cupcake was invented in 1796," Amy says, not looking up.

Riley's eyes are on me.

"Oh," I say. "I work in a biochemistry lab, like a real one, and so I have a lot of experiments and appointments and discoveries to make this weekend—"

"It's not this weekend, silly," she says.

"Uh . . ." I scramble to write an SOP in my head. *How to Avoid*—

"It's next week. My mom needs to be at the bakery on weekends, so she's having her tasting next Thursday after school."

"After-school parties are the best!" Katherine sings.

"It's mostly for her VIP customers, and probably at least one celebrity," Riley says. "But she said I could invite some friends."

I'm frantically writing an SOP in my notebook: *How to Get Out of a Boring Tea Party with a Known Thief.*

"I think my great-aunt is visiting from Hungary," I announce, according to *Step 1: Blame your great-aunt from Hungary.* "Just that day. So I'll probably have to stay home."

*Step 2. Blame your mom, too.*

"My great-aunt's allergic to cupcakes, so my mom would get really mad if I had anything to do with a cupcake party."

*Step 3. Have a pretend dentist appointment to top it all off.*

"Plus, I have to go to the dentist."

"You go to the dentist a lot," bigmouth Katherine-with-a-K says. "I just saw you there a few weeks ago."

I take a spoonful of yogurt, feeling relieved when the conversation turns from my dental hygiene to Timothy's latest dinosaur facts. Even if my pretend great-aunt from Hungary isn't visiting, Elizabeth and I will probably be coordinating packing lists for the Snoozatarium. Our motto is "Be prepared for everything!" And being prepared for everything takes days and days of planning.

Katherine-with-a-K and Timothy have gym next and talk about their various injuries, while Amy keeps reading and ignoring us all. I don't say anything about my catastrophic collision with a soccer ball the other day.

Riley is fishing around in a baggie. "Found it!" A gummy bear is perched between her fingers. "Red. My favorite."

"Red is my favorite," I say for some unknown reason. Because red is not my favorite at all. Green is.

"You can have it." Riley thrusts the bear in my face. "I know how hard it is to find a good red gummy bear these days."

If it was a normal day and I was following standard operating procedures for how to be polite, I would have let her keep her red gummy bear. But today is not a normal day.

I eat it. And I don't even feel bad.

# sixteen

AFTER SCHOOL on Friday, Elizabeth is finally exactly where I hoped I'd find her.

"I have news of genomic proportions," I say, pushing my backpack onto our library table.

"Really?" She offers me a stash of jelly beans.

"You're not going to believe it."

There's a knock on the door to our little room and Elizabeth pops out of her seat to open it. A girl wearing the same uniform as Elizabeth comes in, red-faced, as though she ran all the way here. "Sorry I'm late," she sputters. "Had to meet with my tutor first."

Elizabeth takes her backpack. "Maddie, this is my new friend. I told her about our library after-school thing, and she wants to start coming." They are also wearing matching headbands.

I close my mouth so fast I accidentally bite my tongue. So hard, I feel like crying.

"Grace, this is my old friend Madeline. But you can

call her Maddie." Old friend? I am not the *old* friend. I am the *best* friend.

Grace shakes my hand, which is limp. "Hi! I've heard about all the fun things you guys do together, and guess what? I have a science collection too! Mostly I like to collect rocks and cool gems and—"

"You have a rock collection?" I look at Elizabeth, who knows very well my feelings on rock collectors.

"Like, a really huge one."

And then there is silence, and I'm sure Elizabeth wishes I was easier to get along with right at this moment. But I don't feel like getting along with this fast-talking girl who knows nothing about real science collecting.

"Let's sit down," Elizabeth says, pulling Grace by the arm. "Tell us your huge news, Maddie!"

Grace sits next to me. "You have big news?"

I talk in code, looking at Elizabeth. "Remember that list we were on all summer for the very important event we've been dying to go to?"

Elizabeth sits up straighter. "The Snoozatarium?"

"My dad got us tickets!" I stand up to do our happy dance, which we save for only the best and biggest things, but Elizabeth is still sitting, staring at Grace.

"Aren't we already going to that?" Grace says.

My brain is buzzing and I sit back down. "You're going?

And you didn't tell me?" I clear my throat and start stuffing everything back into my backpack. I have to get out of here.

Elizabeth grabs for me. "Wait, Maddie." But I pull away. She keeps looking at Grace, and this is something I can't stand—because it means secrets, and people don't leave their best friends out of secrets.

"I wanted to tell you, but—"

"That's my birthday, you know." I stop to see what she has to say for herself. And also, she never gave me that new friendship pencil she said she had for me, and maybe now I know why.

"I have to go with school. The entire grade is going together." Elizabeth is trying to pull my backpack away from me. "Just stop. Listen."

"It's no big deal," Grace tells me. "You'll see her there."

"Do you have anyone else who can use the ticket?" Elizabeth says.

"Of course I do. I have like a thousand new friends who are dying to go to the Snoozatarium with me."

"Oh. Good, then," Elizabeth says, and she's twirling her hair like she does when she's upset.

The buzz is in my ears now. I hear myself say, "I didn't actually want to go with you anyway."

"Stop it, Maddie." Elizabeth stands up, turning pink

and looking like maybe she's trying not to cry, and I wish I could take it back. Except Grace is standing next to her now and they're both looking at me like I'm some kind of monster. A bubble of something ugly and burning settles in my chest. I grab my backpack too fast and it falls to the floor. Something shatters, and I pretend not to notice.

"Ew!" Grace says. "What is that smell?"

My petri dish sample from the bus floor ended up growing so fast and so putrid, I stuck it in my bag, quadruple-sealed, to deliver to the lab myself. And now I'm pretty sure it's not quadruple-sealed anymore.

I cough, trying hard not to breathe through my nose. "Also, I can't come to the library from now on because I have a job at a very important lab making very important discoveries. So I hope you don't miss me, because you won't be seeing me anymore."

"Well, maybe she won't," Grace says, her arms crossed.

"Neither will I, and maybe she should just forget we were ever friends!"

"Done!" Grace says. Elizabeth isn't looking at me. Maybe she is crying.

"Fine!" I yell back. "Enjoy your new best friend who's so perfect to get along with, Elizabeth!"

I kick the door open, letting it crash closed behind me, the sound vibrating through the quiet library stacks. It's just like I thought. Just like I wrote in my SOP. *If you get another bad sign the next time you see her, then maybe your best friend isn't your best friend anymore.*

The crisp air does little to cool me down or mask the odor wafting from my bag as I march across the quad. I hate this year. Best friends who stop acting like best friends. Wishing Grandpa were still here all the time. Everything about being eleven-almost-twelve.

The quad is dotted with sprawled-out college kids. Is that all they do? Read in the sun all day? I have to get out of middle school.

"Hey!" someone shouts. "How's your face?"

It's Dexter Sully. I don't stop because there's finally a rhythm to my marching and stomping, and I want to concentrate on being angry and friendless and hard to get along with.

"Madeline, right?" He's got a soccer ball and he dribbles up next to me. "Whoa. Do you smell that?"

"If you want your shirt back, I don't have it," I say, my bag feeling heavy on my back.

He sends the ball directly into my path. Is he trying to give me another bloody nose?

"Kick it," he says.

"Why are you guys always here on campus?" I say. "You're not in college, you know."

"Our coach teaches here. We meet him here for practice."

My whole body feels hot and I'm not sure if I'm going to burst into tears or have a catastrophic nosebleed.

"Kick the ball," Dexter says.

I step over the ball, making sure to clear it with both feet. He pushes the ball out in front of me again. How can Brooke even like this guy? He's annoying.

"Just one good kick. You can't let this soccer ball have the last word."

"I don't like sports," I say, shifting my backpack, which sends out another poof of vomitous stench. "I'm a scientist."

He kicks the ball a little bit. "What? You can't do anything except science?" He smell-checks his shirt, trying to find the source of the stink. I feel my face get red.

Dexter dribbles back up to me, smiling. "Last chance." We're at the other side of the quad now, in front of the stallion statue that Grandpa named Hercules. He would pat the horse's back three times every day for good luck on his way to the lab.

I drop my bag at the base of Hercules, pat his back three times, and wind up.

"Eyes on the ball," he says.

No fancy steps, no calculated angles; I just blow that

ball clear across the quad. It sails wildly left, hitting a tree. But Dexter throws his arms up. "Bam!" he says, nearly knocking me over with his high-five.

And then I pick up my backpack, which doesn't seem so heavy anymore, and walk the rest of the way to my lab.

# Seventeen *

*              *

$D$AD'S IN HIS OFFICE, a stack of papers in front
of him. I drop my backpack onto the floor with a *thunk*.

"That's a lot of books," Dad says, looking up. "And
what is that —"

Before he can finish, I pull the shattered petri dish out
of my backpack and hand it to him.

"Wow. That is potent," he says, cupping his mouth and
nose with his other hand. I gag as he passes by me. In the
lab outside his office, he deposits the bag into a biohazard
bin, the kind with a lid that should be stink-proof. Still, I
try to remember the smell: part decomposed fish at the
edge of a pond, part kitchen sink when our garbage dis-
posal broke right after we stuffed it full of egg casserole.
As soon as I get home, I'll have to record that in my microbiology binder.

"Good news today," Dad says, coming back into the office. "Our enzyme is on its way. Stuck in customs, but on
the way."

"What enzyme?" I say.

Dad stretches, reaching for his lab coat. "A critical component to our project. Really expensive and delicate, but we managed to find enough money in our budget to get a small supply. It's necessary for keeping our grant money. Our investors need to see more forward momentum." He buttons himself up, checking his pockets for his goggles. "And if all goes well, it'll be Hawaii here we come! This family will celebrate with the best vacation ever."

"Can we stay there forever?" I ask, hopeful.

Dad pats me on the head. "It will feel like forever."

No soccer balls or crowded cafeterias. No ex–best friends or weird lunch table not-friends. Hawaii will be total paradise.

We walk over to the corner of the lab, where two giant freezers whir and click. The digital read-outs say negative 80 degrees Celcius in green glow. Colder than Antarctica. Dad grabs a lab chair, wheels it over to a benchtop, and hands me a lab coat. I put it on, rolling the sleeves up, and see that Dad taped my name onto the front of it.

"Is this just-only mine?" I'm never taking this off. I don't even care when I hear Tyrone snort from the sink, where he's washing beakers.

Dad takes out a paper folded in half and props it on

the bench in front of me. It says MADELINE LITTLE, LAB ASSISTANT in very professional letters.

"Everyone who works in my lab needs a nameplate." He grins. "Always keep your goggles on no matter what, and use these gloves to take out the trays in the freezer." He smacks two big clownlike gloves on my bench. *My bench.* I say it again in my head just to remind the rest of my body that it's my bench. Who needs friends when you have your own lab bench?

I take a seat on my stool and spin it around. The lab's a blur of incubators, tubes, glass cylinders, and giant thumping machines. And then my dad's face.

"Ice bucket." He pats the empty container in front of me; it looks like an overgrown red flower pot. "And this is our ice chest." He opens the chest on the floor and scoops out ice with a giant spoon, pouring it into my bucket. Clouds poof up around the ice. "Dry ice," he says. "Don't touch. You'll get frostbite."

"Instant frostbite?" I say. Because not only do I have my own nametag, lab coat, and bench, but I get to work with dry ice, which is very dangerous. I bet Elizabeth and Grace never get to work with dry ice. I bet Riley the Thief doesn't even know what it is.

Dad pulls out some pens and a stack of paper with

*Inventory* written at the top. "Take one tray at a time out of the freezer," Dad says, "place it on the dry ice, and write down the contents of each tray on this paper. Then put the tray back in the freezer and, when you're finished, bring me the inventory sheet so I can file it."

I open my lab notebook. "I need to write all of this down." I start an SOP on *How to Inventory Very Important Scientific Things.*

A high-pitched *beep-beep-beep* rings through the lab and Dad stands up. "The autoclave," he says. "You'll be okay?"

I wave him off, already writing *Step 2: When handling deadly dry ice, proceed with caution and do not tell your mother.*

By the time Dad is finished with work, I've managed to inventory thirty-nine science things, including one liter of rabbit blood, twenty-four bottles of high-salt buffer, something labeled *Blue Sepharose* that was dark as ink but also sandy-looking, and a bunch of tiny tubes labeled with numbers and letters. I'm so fast that this is probably an inventory record.

"Good job, sweetie," Dad says, helping me pack up before the walk home. We leave the dry ice to evaporate in its bucket overnight. If you pour it into the sink, the pipes will freeze and crack and cause mass destruction, a fact I quickly write in my notebook and may or may not share with know-it-all Riley.

It's getting darker a little earlier now. The athletic fields have their lights on, and I'm relieved when Dad doesn't take the shortcut through soccer practice. Grandpa's house, dark and silent, looms in front of us when we turn onto Main Street. His car is still parked in the driveway, now with a For Sale sign in the back window.

"Thinking of getting the U-Haul this week," Dad says. "There's a thrift store in Milton that will take anything."

This is a topic I do not want to hear about.

"For everything that didn't go in the estate sale," Dad continues. "It's got to be cleared out before we put the house up for sale and have the first open house."

I cross my arms against the fall chill. How can we just throw Grandpa's stuff into a thrift shop? So people can buy his little trinkets and toss them in their junk drawers? Dad says I don't understand, and how are we supposed to deal with a house full of so many things accumulated over a lifetime? We hardly even have space for Mom's yoga mats at home.

So I write an SOP in my head to try to salvage the tiny happiness from my first day in the lab after another hard day at school and an even harder time at the library: *How to Change the Subject in One Simple Step.*

*Step 1. Distract the person by asking unnecessary questions.*

"Hey, Dad, can you tell me where Ursa Major is again?" I say, staring into the night sky.

Dad points. "Right there."

"I don't see it."

"Follow my finger," he says, pointing while opening Grandpa's mailbox with his other hand. Just some junk mail.

"Don't see it," I say, looking up.

Dad shuts the mailbox and points again. "Right there, with the Big Dipper, remember?"

And all the rest of the walk home, he points over and over to the cluster of stars that makes Ursa Major, the first constellation I ever saw when I was little.

# eighteen

WHEN I GET HOME, I run up to my room and pull my bag of swabs out of my backpack. I have three today: from a dollar I got as change at the school store, from a tambourine in the music room, and from a soccer cleat in the lost and found. I check my petri dishes from yesterday, and the rock moss sample is growing well, already speckled with greenish fuzz. The bus window dish from earlier this week is still pretty empty; just a few glossy dots of yellow.

I pull out *Bergey's Manual* and compare the yellow dots to one of the pictures in the book. Candida. A fungus. I'll let it grow for a few more days before I take pictures and log it in my microbiology binder.

Next I put on my sterile lab gloves so I don't get my own germs on my swab samples, then take the stinky soccer cleat swab out of its bag. I lift the lid of the first petri dish and zigzag the swab across the agar. Then I label it, close the lid, and wrap it with tape before doing the next one. After they're all stacked safely in the corner of my closet for incubation, I tromp down the stairs with a pile of books.

"Brooke, I think you have a bloody nose," Dad says, loading the dishwasher.

Mom runs into the kitchen for paper towels, nearly clobbering me. Brooke wipes her nose and finds a smear of red on her hand. "Well, this is just great!" she yells from the couch, where she's watching her favorite show, *Say Yes to the Prom Dress*.

"Not the carpet! Not the carpet!" Mom pulls off a wad of paper towel and pushes it against Brooke's nose. I drop my books on the table, start my timer, and go to hold her hair back, but it's already pulled into a ponytail. "Madeline, we need more paper towels," Mom calls. "Ice, too."

I grab more towels and reach into the freezer for the dinosaur Boo-Boo Buddy we've had since we were babies. "More ice than that, Maddie," Dad says. "Keep pinching your nose, Brooke."

"Is it on me?" she cries. "This is like my favorite shirt. Did I get it on me?"

After seven minutes, I ask, "Should I get my nasal spray?" but Mom shakes her head. The spray doesn't work for Brooke. She's one step from self-infusion, Dad told me, which means she would have to use a needle at home to get her medicine. Even though we have the same type of Von Willebrand disease, Brooke's is more severe.

I sit down at the kitchen table and watch my timer. My student handbook is there, and on the inside page is a picture of a bunch of kids, all laughing and super smiley. But can they really be best friends, all of them, all the time? Because eventually, as everyone knows, maybe your friends will change from being your friends. And then you'll be going to a Snoozatarium alone on your birthday.

"Maybe you should come by the lab and we'll draw some blood," Dad tells Brooke when the bleeding finally stops. He grabs her medical logbook. "Have you been getting more nosebleeds lately?"

Brooke says, "Nope." And then she goes down to her room, a roll of paper towels tucked under her arm.

Mom sighs and sits in her rocking chair under the naked lady and starts winding organic wool into one of her dryer balls. "Pre-orders are pouring in. There are only two weeks left to make all of these, plus what I want to sell at the festival."

"Pumpkin Fest is the same day as the Snoozatarium?"

"And your birthday. It will be a full Saturday."

"Maybe I should skip the Snoozatarium, then." I picture us, Dad and me, trying out the tornado simulator while Elizabeth stands in line with the kids from her school, all of them laughing and being best friends and wondering why I didn't bring a friend of my own. And what if it's because Elizabeth is right? Am I really not as fun and easy to get along with as I thought?

"Don't be ridiculous. You have to go." Mom ties off the end of a dryer ball and stuffs it into one foot of a pair of pantyhose, knotting the hose just above the ball. When she has three or four balls tied in a row, she'll put them through the washing machine and dryer over and over again until the balls are soft and felted. "Can you go get the batch in the dryer? Just bring them all up. There's a laundry basket on your sister's bed."

"Isn't Brooke down there?" I say.

"Just knock first," Mom says, already winding a new ball.

I make as much noise as possible, creaking all the steps on the way down, and then jumping on the last step in the perfectly right spot for an especially loud squeak in order to avoid surprising an angry Brooke Little.

The laundry room door swings open. "What?" Brooke's face is puffy and swollen from her nosebleed.

"I know you lied to Dad," I say. "And you're not updating your logbook."

Brooke rolls her eyes. "Mom and Dad would overreact, and then Coach would pull me off stunts." She shakes her head. "Too close to the Pumpkin Tournament." She disappears into the laundry room and behind a sheet she's hung from the ceiling.

I peek inside. She's created her own little curtained-off bedroom down here, separate from the rest of the basement.

"Where'd you find that?" It's an actual twin bed. On wheels.

She hops up and pulls her pillow off. "It's an old-timey cot we had stored down here." She folds the bed in half and then flips it back to full size again. "Pretty comfortable, actually."

It's covered with stuffed pandas, of course. So are the upside-down pail she's using for a bedside table and the drying rack her clothes are hanging on. My big sister collects pandas obsessively. I've been looking for an anonymous hotline to turn her in for hoarding, but so far I haven't found one.

"There's a lot of junk down here," I say, pulling the sheet back. And I don't just mean Brooke's thousand or so pandas. I mean the Rollerblades hanging from the ceiling, the dog bowls stacked in the corner for the dog we never got, and the dusty skis leaning up against the rack full of canned beans and peaches. Half the stuff cluttering this area, we never even use. I look at the cracked concrete floor and the spider-webby beams on the ceiling.

"At least it doesn't smell like rotting-corpse petri dishes down here," Brooke says.

"Aren't there a ton of bugs?" Mom is against any kind of pest control. She says the chemicals mess with hormones and give people cancer, an opinion that is seriously unfortunate when you have an infestation.

"You're such a baby about bugs." Brooke shakes her head. "I'm tougher than you."

"It's not about toughness; it's about hygiene and safety and intelligence," I say. "Bugs harbor disease, and some of them have sharp enough teeth to eat an entire shoe."

"Then you would hate the spider crickets." Brooke sits back on her bed and pulls out a nail file.

"Spider what?" I say, grabbing the dryer balls out of the dryer. They're still knotted in their pantyhose, looking like giant beads, all soft and felted after several cycles of washing and drying.

"Half spider, half cricket," Brooke says. "As soon as the lights go out. Thousands of them."

"Shut up," I say, heading fast through the door with my basket of wool balls. "You would never sleep down here if that were true. You're such a liar."

"Am I?" she says. "Hey, look! There's one now!"

I rush out of the room, tripping on the stairs, Brooke laughing behind me.

# nineteen

I SPEND THE REST of the weekend in the lab, avoiding the library and writing up an SOP on *How to Find a New Best Friend*.

*Step 1. Hmm.*

*Step 2. Um.*

*Step 3. Think! Think! Think!*

Even worse, at school on Monday, Katherine-with-a-K catches me swabbing an old sock in the locker room lost and found and tells everyone in the entire universe. And then in gym, because I keep somehow kicking the ball into the thorny bushes, I earn myself the not-nice nickname Hook Foot. At this rate, it's pretty much like I'll never have friends in middle school. Especially not in science class, because nobody in my group has even heard of symbiosis.

By Wednesday, I don't even care anymore. I don't laugh when the teacher makes a nematode joke in science, or raise my hand to show my work on the board in math. At lunch, I'm extra quiet. I eat my sandwich and write in my lab notebook, ignoring Amy flipping through her encyclopedia beside me. She eats a yellow-cheese and mustard sandwich, which she does every day, chewing with her mouth open and making lots of smacking sounds.

*How to Tell a Person Eating a Yellow-Cheese and Mustard Sandwich to Close her Mouth.*

*Step 1. Tell her there is a fly buzzing around and you'd hate to see her swallow it even though flies aren't deathly poisonous.*

*Step 2. Tell her that you've heard flies taste a lot like sweaty socks and soccer cleats.*

*Step 3. Remind her that flies like to eat dog poop and horse poop and all sorts of other poop.*

Katherine-with-a-K snorts when she sees Amy reading about the kookaburra. "K-O-O-K-A-B-U-R-R-A!" she sings. If she were a real friend, I might even congratulate her on spelling such a hard word. But then she gets quiet and serious again, shuffling through her word cards.

"Ever see anything in there on spider crickets?" I ask Amy, but she only shakes her head, reading.

Riley picks the olives out of her salad. "Don't forget my cupcake party is tomorrow. Lots of yummy food from the best baker in town. My mom, of course."

I give her the stink-eye according to my SOP on *How to Send a Warning Signal with Body Language Alone*, which I conveniently thought up last night and promptly recorded on page thirty of my lab notebook.

Riley sighs and I wonder why she's always bragging. Probably because she's been lying all along about her astronaut buddies. She probably doesn't even know any astronauts at all, and now she's going to fail Independent Study.

I write an SOP on *How to Spot a Liar*.

*Step 1. She has no problem stealing things from old people's houses.*

*Step 2. She pretends she got her Space Camp necklace from Space Camp, but maybe it's from the Internet.*

*Step 3. A lot of liars are named Riley.*

"What are you writing about, anyway, Madeline?" Riley says.

"Very important scientific observations and conclusions," I say.

"Can I see?"

I slam my notebook closed. Everyone at the table looks up. My book is already half-full of SOPs: *How to Survive*

*Lunch at a Table of Misfit Know-It-Alls. How to Avoid Unwanted Conversations. How to Look Like You're Listening Even When You're Not.*

I hide my notebook in my backpack, because honestly, my SOPs sound kind of mean. I decide to write SOP fifty-six when I get home: *How to Give to the Poor and Stuff.*

"I'd have to talk to NASA and my dad before I let anyone read my notebook," I say. "My discoveries are highly classified."

"That makes sense," Riley says. "I'd be careful with my science notebook too, if I had one."

For the rest of the day, I think hard about my SOPs compared to Grandpa's. His SOPs were for things like *How to Make the Mailman Smile,* because Grandpa wanted to remember that his favorite kind of cookie was peanut butter and that he loved penguins and thank-you cards. When Grandpa was really tired, we'd sit on his couch and write SOPs all day about how to work the TV or how to charge his cell phone or how to make someone happy.

By the time the bell rings at the end of school, my whole body feels heavy with shame. And then I hear a familiar and terrifying voice in the hall.

"Maddie Maddie Bo-Baddie, Banana-ana Fo-Faddie!"

My mother.

I cringe. "Shhh!" But more than a few people turn

around as they file out of school to the buses. It doesn't help that Mom is rolling a giant wire ball, knocking into trash cans and lockers. She bends to pick it up, but the ball keeps rolling, building speed. Mom runs after it, her shoes clip-clopping and her eco-friendly hemp jacket flying out behind her like a cape.

I remember what Dexter said—keep your eye on the ball—so when the wire ball is within range of my foot, I kick it back up to Mom. It sails over a backpack in the middle of the hall and lands at Mom's feet. "Wow, Madeline." She picks the ball up. "Nice kick."

"It's only two thirty." I know why she's here: EcoKids. "No after-school activities until three. You're early."

Mom waves me off. "Better early than late."

I look both ways down the hallway, thankful most kids have left for home, and pull her onto a bench away from the lockers. "What is that, anyway?" I say.

Mom puts the gigantic wire ball between her feet and her bag between us. "Mother Earth." I wonder if Brooke knows just how convenient it is that she has cheerleading practice and can't come to EcoKids.

"What did Elizabeth say about the ticket?" Mom asks. "Was she ecstatic?"

"I haven't told her yet," I lie. "No time. We're both super busy and stuff."

"Is she too busy to come, you think?"

I write an SOP in my head on *How to Get Your Mom to Stop Asking So Many Questions.*

"I think you need a tissue," I say, according to *Step 1: Tell her she has a booger.*

She whips a tissue out of her bag and wipes her nose without even taking a breath. "Maybe you should start thinking of another friend to take with you?"

*Step 2. Tell her it's still there.*

Mom lugs her bag onto her lap and pulls out her mirror. "I don't see it. Anyway, what about the new girl? I hear she's having a cupcake party tomorrow. I think you should go." Mom fishes around in her bag and holds up Riley's invitation.

*Step 3. Tell her there is a tarantula-looking spider in her hair.*

I don't. Because that would be mean. How'd I get so mean, anyway? Instead I say, "Where'd you get that? There's no way in a million years I'm going."

Mom rubs my back, but I shrug her off because I'm mean now. It's not even my fault. Elementary school is all playgrounds and pinecone bird feeders. Middle school doesn't even let you spend your lunch in the library. What do they expect? I'm a product of my environment.

"Sweetheart," Mom says, almost whispering. "Grandpa

will always live in our hearts." She pats her chest. "Right here."

What does any of this have to do with Grandpa? I stand up. I've heard this speech one thousand and fifty million times. No, actually, he is not living anymore. Anyone with half a brain knows he's not living. Because that's what happens when someone dies. They are gone, and they are gone *forever.*

"Grandpa would want to see you making friends and trying really hard in middle school. He'd want to see you at that party."

"Honestly, he wouldn't care about a stupid cupcake party. Also, I'm sure Grandpa doesn't want you to sell his house. So that's not very nice."

Mom sighs too loud. "We can't keep the house, Madeline. It needs too much work that we can't afford. You know that."

I check my nose because my blood is feeling extra hot, and it would be just my luck to get a nosebleed in the middle of the school hallway, sitting with Mom and her Mother Earth. "It's part of our family history."

Mom shakes her head. "Sometimes you've got to let go of things, sweetie. I'll tell you what, though." She pats my leg. "With school just starting and the Pumpkin Fest and your birthday coming up, maybe we should talk to Dad about shifting the open house date a bit later."

"Really?" I sit back down.

"Just a few weeks," Mom says. "Maybe everyone will be able to think more clearly."

I wipe my nose one more time. Still clean.

"We could go over there together and make sure there's nothing left that you'd like to keep before we do the final pack-up. Dad might appreciate the break, too."

I don't like the words *final pack-up*, but I give Mom a quick hug. Even though she spends her free time winding wool balls and making Mother Earths that look more like strange wire sculptures, sometimes she can be a little bit nice.

# TWENTY

I DON'T RESIST going with Mom to her after-school program now that we've had our talk about the house. I know we'll still have to sell it eventually, but a tiny glimmer of hope is all I can ask for. I'll even sing the "EcoKids! EcoKids! We love Mother Earth! EcoKids! EcoKids! We know what she's worth!" chant that Mom wrote and rewrote fifty thousand times last night.

"I have to stop at the little girls' room," Mom says on our way to the classroom, a bit too loudly.

"Okay," I say. And then she hands me the wire ball, which I balance on my hip so I can drag her thousand-pound bag, stuffed full of magazines and newspapers and a smaller bag of loose wire. "I'll meet you in the room," I say, pointing down the hall. I am not about to wait here and cause an EcoKids spectacle.

When I arrive, I'm shocked to find two other girls waiting. I didn't think anyone would come. "Are you here for EcoKids?"

They nod. One girl is wearing what looks like a fur jacket.

"Are you wearing fur?" I let my wire ball roll away from me and nestle between the desk and trash can. If you're a true EcoPerson like my mother, fur is unacceptable.

"It's made from recycled soda can rings and diapers."

I grimace, and the other girl, who is wearing an ordinary sweater vest and practical penny loafers, moves her chair noisily away from Fur Girl.

"EcoKids! EcoKids! We love Mother Earth! EcoKids! EcoKids! We know what she's worth!" Mom sings. Her entrance is probably the entire reason for her visit to the bathroom. "EcoKids! EcoKids! We love Mother Earth—" She gives me a look like *Join in!* but instead her giant bag accidentally slides off my shoulder and smacks hard on the tile floor, making her lose her place in the chant.

"We know what she's worth!" I finish.

The other girls clap, and Mom, who probably planned on chanting until half the school joined in, bows and smiles.

"Thank you, thank you," Mom says, glowing. "And welcome, fellow EcoKids! You've chosen a challenging and important after-school club, and I applaud you for that." She claps her hands, and Fur Girl and Penny Loafers fake-bow.

"Is that Fur the Love of the Planet fur?" Mom says, reaching for the fur cuff on Fur Girl's shirt.

"Yes, it is!" she says.

"Fantastic!" Mom pets her. "Madeline, it's made from diapers. Amazing, right?"

"Amazing," I say, feeling the energy fizzling right out of me. I should be studying, getting ready to make a new lab discovery that would baffle and awe my dad and Tyrone. Everyone would wonder how in the world such a genius scientist had been overlooked for so long. They'd —

"Did you hear me, Madeline? Go get some wire," Mom's saying.

I notice that the other girls are huddled around the bag of wire, pulling out strands. When it's my turn, all I find is a jumble of wire fragments.

"This is an abstract exercise," Mom says. "No rules. No limitations." She rolls the giant wire ball over and holds it in place with the tip of her shoe. "This is our Mother Earth. Before we papier-mâché her, I'd like each of you to add something that has meaning for you. Sculpt it from the leftover wire. Let's not waste anything."

I know exactly what I'll make. I take my jumble and massage it until the wires break away from one another. I sculpt and squeeze, and before long my bunch of junk takes shape, turning into a Von Willebrand molecule.

Maybe there's a bit of Grandpa's artistic skill in me. I put my sculpture on my placemat and take out my notebook while I wait for everyone to catch up. I write an SOP on *How to Be Friendly.*

*Step 1. Smile like you just heard that joke about the amoeba that accidentally ate a paramecium.*

*Step 2. Ask someone if she's looking for a best friend because you have an opening and have recently improved yourself in the "getting along" department.*

*Step 3. Tell someone you like her socks.*

The other girls take nearly the entire EcoKids time, they're working so hard.

"Time's up, everyone!" Mom says. "Great job. I see you both made trees. How wonderful!" Fur Girl and Penny Loafers hold up their pieces of art, and when I squint my eyes, I see it. I can see their trees and, actually, they're beautiful. Fur Girl even added baby birds in a wire nest. Penny Loafers' tree has apples ready for picking.

I look at my molecule. "Great job, honey," Mom says, rubbing her hands together the way she does when she's uncomfortable. She has no idea what I've made.

"I made a tree, too," I say quickly, my face heating up. My molecule looks nothing like a tree. Actually, it doesn't even look much like a molecule.

"They have trees like this in Hawaii," Mom says.

Middle school is making all of us a bunch of liars. "Nice root system, Madeline."

The other girls get up and add their perfect trees to the wire Mother Earth. Mom pulls my molecule tree away from me and attaches it carefully to the wire ball. She can't get it to stay upright. It looks more like a sideways decapitated snowman, about to destroy the earth with its melting snow.

"Next meeting, we papier-mâché!" Mom says with a flourish.

When the girls get up to leave and turn their backs to pack their bags, I swab Fur Girl's dirty-diaper collar. Mom frowns at me. I ignore her, and as soon as she looks away, I peel my decapitated snowman off Mother Earth and throw it in the trash.

It's like the only thing I'm good at is science. Everything else just turns out to be a mess.

# TWENTY-ONE

ON THE DRIVE HOME, Mom swings into the university library parking lot to drop me off. "Be home before dusk, and please watch out for soccer balls and anything else." She kisses me on the cheek and I get out of the car like the library is exactly what I have in mind. Like it's just a normal day and my best friend is waiting inside to study with me. I walk into the library so my mom thinks everything's the same, but my gut does not like this plan. Probably food poisoning, or something worse — yellow fever mixed with the black plague.

I trudge up the main stairs, passing clusters of college kids with shoulder bags and smiles and enough friends for dozens of Snoozatarium tickets. I creep into the art history stacks because I just want to peek in, to see if Elizabeth still comes. To see if life is the same for her when I'm not in it.

My skin is getting hot again, my backpack heavy, and even though my nose is dry, I feel the blood gathering where it shouldn't be, like I'm ready to make a scene. I write an SOP in my head on *How to Stop Being a Stalker-Weirdo.*

*Step 1. Go home.*

*Step 2. Admit defeat.*

*Step 3. Tell Mom everything.*

I don't listen to myself, and when I stand on my tiptoes to look through the little window in the door, nobody is there. But the table is stacked with books, and two backpacks are flung over the chairs. One is Grace's; I remember the pink and purple flowers globbed all over it. The other one is Elizabeth's: practical, blue and silver, sparkly like the ceiling of the planetarium.

If Grandpa were in charge of writing my SOPs, he'd say, *Step 1. Find her.*

*Step 2. Make amends.*

*Step 3. Get along.*

But I'm not Grandpa. My whole body feels fiery, and I have to leave. Fast, so I don't run into them.

It's now the late-afternoon library rush and the stairway is clogged with college students. I flatten myself against the railing, but my backpack gets bumped, bumped, bumped. I remember that I stuffed my pencil box into the tiny pocket on the outside of my bag, and when I reach for it, it falls. And then the crowd parts and everything gets quiet except for the *click, click, click* of pencils bouncing and clattering down the stairs. People are catching them, dodging them, tripping and sliding on them. And I must look like such a middle-schooler, because when the students pick them up they automatically hand them to me, with all their rainbows, peace signs, and kittens.

I take a few and rush downstairs. When I turn around, pencils are still scattered, and Elizabeth and Grace are standing at the top of the stairs looking right at me.

I do exactly the opposite of what Grandpa would've done. I leave. One of the college kids grabs my shirt. "Here's another," she says. And she's holding the nub of the smiley-face friendship pencil Elizabeth gave me last year.

"It's not mine," I lie.

Elizabeth, the traitor of all traitors, watches me as I walk away. Mom's right. Sometimes you just have to let things go.

The lab is the only place I feel like I belong anymore. Tyrone is sitting at his bench in flip-flops and shorts, like it's not completely against the lab rules and fifty degrees outside. "Just watering the flowers," he jokes, filling a giant vat with water from a hose in the sink. "Hey, where's my ticket to the Snoozatarium? Your dad says the whole place will sing 'Happy Birthday' to you. My parents gave me a surprise party when I was twelve. There were trampolines and a dog show. The kind where dogs jump through hoops and over logs and stuff. So fun. And then all the neighborhood kids —"

I can't even manage a smile. I just shrug into my lab coat and push on my goggles. The autoclave chirps and I jump up. "I'll get it!"

I grab my notebook, snap on some latex gloves, and walk down the hallway to the autoclave room. It's quiet from my side of the door, and for some reason, I knock before I swing the door open and look inside. He's all sweaty and steamed up, a red light flashing from his read-out panel. I shuffle closer, keeping the door open in case I need to make a fast escape, and then he chirps again. The read-out panel says CYCLE COMPLETE. And then a high-pitched, eardrum-breaking siren fills the room. I whirl around, looking for the autoclave's SOP, my eye catching the big red button on the wall that says SILENT. I pound it with my fist and the world returns to its normal hum, with a new, slightly distracting buzz to go with it.

I sit in Dad's chair. "Bad boy," I say. But the autoclave doesn't care about eardrums or bad days or panic attacks. He just purrs from his place on the wall.

This room is almost as bleak as Brooke's basement bedroom. The autoclave needs some pictures, some decorations, maybe even a window to look out. He doesn't even get any visitors except for my dad and Tyrone. And Dad's always yelling at him and pushing his buttons and forcing his giant teeth open. "You need a friend, Autoclave," I say. "You can come to my birthday if you want. I have an extra ticket, you know."

As I pick up my notebook and pen, the autoclave chirps at me, and in my obviously disturbed mind, I pretend he says yes. I make a mental check mark in the box for my new best friend: a giant, lonely dishwasher-sterilizer.

There's going to be a lot of leftover birthday cake this year.

## TWENTY-TWO

MR. SID IS HEAVING a giant pumpkin onto his front porch when I get home. "How's it going, Mr. Sid?" I ask from the sidewalk.

He turns, his hands on his hips, out of breath. "Good news! I got nominated for the Pumpkin Festival garden tour!" His garden is mostly dark burgundies, oranges, and yellows right now, sturdier plants that look like they'd survive a trampling or two from Bark. Not like in summer, when his front yard is every color of the rainbow, wild with delicate long-necked flowers and baskets of cascading blooms.

"Congratulations," I say, laughing because Mr. Sid is now kissing each flower like a honeybee.

"I've been waiting for this nomination for years." And then he turns back to his front porch and attempts to move his giant pumpkin.

"Hey, dummy." It's my favorite sister coming home, an

overstuffed bag of cheerleading paraphernalia slung over her shoulder.

"Aren't you cold?" She's in her cheerleading T-shirt and shorts. "It's not even sixty degrees out here."

"Nag, nag, nag," she says. "You sound like Mom." Her nose is swollen, I can tell, just a tiny bit.

"Did you have another nosebleed?"

"Blah, blah, blah. Nag, nag, nag."

I hear the familiar snurfling sounds of Bark.

"Oh no, you don't!" Mr. Sid says, dropping his pumpkin with a worrisome *crack* and running toward his front gate.

"Hi, Bark." I lean down to give him a pat.

Mr. Sid is at the sidewalk now, and he grabs the first thing within reach: Brooke's megaphone. "Take your wrinkled bulldog fanny on out of here, Beast!" Mr. Sid makes a police siren noise through the megaphone and Brooke and I cover our ears. Bark just cocks his head and barks, wagging his tail.

Brooke grabs her megaphone back. Mr. Sid is nearly out in the road now, the beast lumbering back home.

"Don't worry, Mr. Sid, you'll get him next time," I say, following Brooke to our house.

Inside, Mom's sitting in the chair under her naked

lady painting as usual, winding away at her dryer balls, looking a bit off-kilter. "Ten more days, girls." She rocks her chair a little faster than usual. "Never had so many pre-orders before."

That means ten more days for me, too. How did my birthday get here so fast?

"Maybe I should just help you at the Pumpkin Fest. Forget about going to the Snoozatarium that night. It's too much." I bite my nails, a habit I thought I'd broken.

Mom stops rocking. "Nonsense. The Pumpkin Fest will be over by four, and then you'll have plenty of time to get to the science museum."

"But maybe Dad has to work on packing Grandpa's house. He'll probably be too tired."

"If Elizabeth can't go . . ." Mom looks at me, and it's like she knows everything. I stare at my bitten nails. "I hope you'll see if Riley can go instead. I can talk to her mother tomorrow when I drop you off at the cupcake tasting."

"What?" There's no way I'm going to that party. "I have to study tomorrow. I am not going."

"You're going."

"I'm not. Her mom probably uses nitrates in her cupcake batter!"

Mom's not buying it. "You're going."

I'm stomping up the stairs to my room when Dad

bursts through the front door. "The enzyme!" He throws his arms wide. "After six months on backorder and three weeks in customs, the enzyme has arrived!"

I hop back down the stairs. "Congratulations, Dad!"

Mom rushes over so we're all hugging at the same time. She says, "Daniel, your father would be so happy."

And I can feel Dad's squeeze weaken. Grandpa knew the lab was in danger of losing its grant money. When Dad learned about the enzyme, Grandpa was pretty forgetful already, but even he knew that it might lead to the discovery they needed to keep the research project going.

"That means you'll get the funding?" Mom says.

Dad nods. "If the results prove what I hope they prove." We break from our clumsy hug.

"And then we're going on vacation?" I say, hoping maybe we can leave before my birthday. We can celebrate under the stars. Hawaiian stars.

"What's going on up here?" Brooke says from the basement steps. "I have a test tomorrow, in case anybody cares."

"Dad's enzyme came in," I say. "We're going to Hawaii."

Her phone buzzes in her hand. "It's about time," she says, and heads back downstairs.

# TWENTY-THREE

EVEN THOUGH ALL I want to do is help Dad in the lab after school, Mom surprises me by showing up at the final bell to drive me over to Riley's cupcake party and abandon me there. She takes my backpack home, but I keep my notebook and favorite pen with me, because as soon as Mom drives around the corner I'm going to ditch the party and find a park bench and write some SOPs. My book's almost entirely full, but there are still a few from Grandpa that I need to write down, and I have more than fifteen new ones on my list. Except Mom's refusing to drive away until I ring the doorbell, even though I've been waving goodbye for a full minute.

A girl in a Three Sisters Bakery WHERE EVERYTHING IS THREE TIMES BETTER! apron opens the door. "Helloooo, and welcome to our Three Sisters cupcake tasting!" She's a Riley look-alike, except taller, with a pointier nose and longer bangs. "You're early. The festivities will start in the backyard in a few minutes. Hope you brought an empty stomach!"

As I step into the house, my mouth waters against my will at the smell of warm vanilla and cake. A Riley look-alike number two wearing a matching apron stands behind the kitchen counter, squirting dollops of pink frosting on mini-cupcakes and topping each of them with a cherry.

"Mom! Cupcake sundaes are finished!" she yells.

"Where's Riley?" A voice comes from a back room. "Tell her to take them out, will you? I'm getting the peppermint ready."

"Riiiiilllllleyyyyyy!" the look-alikes scream in unison.

"And tell her to put her apron on," their mom adds.

I'm creeping through the family room, hoping to get outside and slip through the back gate before anyone else sees me, when a door from the yard flies open. In waltzes Riley wearing a CALL ME A SCIENCE GEEK shirt instead of the bakery apron. She pulls a giant, jowly brown dog in behind her. He collapses onto the tile floor, panting.

"You came!" she says, clapping when she sees me.

"Riley." One of the look-alikes stands in front of us, balancing a tray of sundae cupcakes. "Mom said you have to put your apron on, and also take these out and put them on the serving plate with the banana cream cup-cakes."

"Frederick just ate half a row of oatmeal raisin cup-cakes and then pooped next to the milk station. I picked it up, and maybe got some on my hands." She waves at her sister, who scrambles away like Riley's hand is a fireball from space about to take over the world.

"I'm going to clean up," Riley says, grabbing my hand. "Let's go."

I pull away because I do not want poop on my hands, but her grip is pretty tight.

"Sorry about my sisters," Riley says when we get up-stairs, out of breath. "People take cupcakes very seriously around here, and if you want to know a secret" — she looks down the hallway — "I don't even like cupcakes."

She reaches behind a framed picture of a baby in a diaper holding a cupcake to his chocolate-smeared face. At the bottom it says GOT CUPCAKE? She pulls out a key and unlocks her bedroom door, then returns the key to the frame. "I installed the lock after one of my megalodon shark teeth fossils went missing. I'm sure my sisters took one just to torture me. I'm down to three now."

I have one fossil. A fern leaf. "Do you have poop on your hands? Shouldn't you wash up?"

She laughs, taking a running leap onto the beanbag

chair by her desk. "I just told my sister that. She'll believe anything."

"Are these all your books?" She has all of my favorites: *Fahrenheit 451, The Hot Zone, The Evolution of Calpurnia Tate.* "Have you read them all?"

"At least twice," she says. "But I wanted to show you something else." She reaches down to a low shelf and pulls out a big shoebox. "This is the finest object in all my collections. It's been in my family for a hundred years. My great-grandpa gave it to me on his deathbed. Are you ready?"

I shrug my shoulders, folding my arms over my lab notebook. Riley whips off the lid, revealing a giant round rock.

"Ta-da! It's a meteorite," she squeals. "A real, live, one-of-a-kind meteorite."

I suck in a breath. "But not the real kind, like, from actual space, right?" Because I've never seen one this big outside of a museum case. "Where'd you buy that?"

"No, silly. It's been in my family for a hundred years, remember? Or something like that, anyway." Riley hands me the box. "You can pick it up if you want."

I put my notebook down and take the box, stroking the meteorite. "It's real?"

"It's really, really real." Riley bounces onto the bed

next to me. "My great-great-great grandma found it in her backyard."

The rock feels smooth and heavy and cold to the touch. "Wow," I say, wondering if this is what space feels like. "How did she know it was a meteorite?"

"She watched it fall from the sky," Riley says. "I come from a looooong line of scientists. And my great-great-great grandma had a telescope, which was really rare for the olden days." She hops off the bed. "The meteorite was so hot they couldn't touch it for three days."

I turn it over, feeling its underbelly. "You're so lucky," I say. This would make the ultimate scientific collection.

"I know." Riley flops onto her beanbag. "I knew you'd like it." She pulls a book of microbes off her shelf and I almost tell her about my antique Bunsen burner. "Katherine said you have a lot of science stuff, right?"

"How does Katherine know that?"

"She said you guys have been friends since kindergarten. Friends like that just know things about each other."

Since when does Katherine-with-a-K think I'm her friend?

Riley crosses her legs. "I've never had a good group of friends like the lunch table."

"But they're so . . ." I think for a minute, because Riley seems to really, honestly, genuinely like them. ". . . weird."

Riley laughs. "We're *all* so weird! I mean, I practically live in a cupcake castle, and you collect beakers with holes in them. Everyone in this whole world is weird."

Elizabeth is not weird, and she was the best friend I could have ever had. But when I think harder, I realize that an outsider might not get that Elizabeth only uses pencils because she doesn't want anyone to see her mistakes, or that she carries jelly beans around with her because in kindergarten her mom said they were brain beans. Everyone has something other people might think is weird. Even my sister, who has a ton of friends, is weird about her panda obsession.

Riley interrupts my thoughts. "You're so lucky to have a scientist for a dad."

"But you just said you come from a long line of scientists." I place the meteorite in its box and hand it back.

"Well, the line stops at my mother, who basically hates science." Riley sighs, clutching the box. "She wants me to be a cupcake baker with my sisters. She doesn't even understand why I want to keep this 'old rock,' as she calls it."

Right now, Riley does not look like the know-it-all Space Camp girl from school. Her million clinky bracelets are not even clinking. Riley and her bracelets are just slumped on her beanbag chair.

"My grandpa died of mercury exposure when his lab

thermometer exploded," she says. "He wasn't wearing goggles, and he got some in his eye. My mom was only five."

"Oh." I'm not sure what to say. "My grandpa died too."

"I know." And then we are both quiet.

I look out the window and see that the cupcake tasting party is starting. Amy and Katherine are by the fountain in the backyard, along with a bunch of people gathered around the tables of sweets. Amy looks different without her encyclopedias, but Katherine looks just the same, and is probably being loud and spelling everything.

"I like to grow stuff on petri dishes," I say. "Like swab things and see what grows." That's been true pretty much since fourth grade, when I did an experiment for the science fair and found disgusting bacteria on our kitchen sponge. According to my experiment, microwaving it and then running it through the dishwasher disinfected it completely. I don't say all this out loud, though. It might be *too* weird.

"Cool," Riley says.

So I continue. "I swabbed a soccer cleat from the lost and found last week, and it's already growing big puffs of nasty stuff." Strange hobby, I guess."

"Nothing is strange in the name of science." Riley

stands up, looking outside. She bangs on her window, waving to Katherine and Amy. "Hey. Have any swabs with you right now?"

I nod. I never go anywhere without a swab or two.

"You're going to love this." She pulls me out of the room.

"Wait, my notebook."

"It's okay. I always lock up."

Riley uses her key from the frame again and we tiptoe down the hall, checking behind us, being super secretive. She stops. "My sister's room." She opens the door really slowly, and even slower through the creaks. It's like she's done this a hundred times.

Once we're inside, she points to something on the bedside table, and I creep in for a closer look. It's a retainer.

"I know for a fact she never washes it," Riley whispers.

I grin, pull two swabs out of my pocket, and hand one to her. I demonstrate how to swab, rubbing the cotton tip on the retainer, and she copies me. And then I'm double careful as I slide them back into their wrappers. Riley gives me a high-five, her bracelets clinking softly, and we sneak back out of the room.

"Thanks for showing me your science collection," I say as we head down the stairs, and I realize that she was hardly braggy at all. And even if she was, it didn't bother me so much.

When we go outside, everyone is lounging around the backyard fountain, chocolate on their lips and fingers. We all sit in a circle and test five different cupcakes, tiny bite-size samples that we pop into our mouths at the same time. And then we shout out a number, one to ten, to rate how much we like each one. Katherine-with-a-K spells out her numbers, of course, and surprisingly, it's kind of funny. Amy has this snorting, hooting kind of laugh that gets everyone giggling. And then it's like I don't even know myself anymore because I can't stop laughing either. I give the cupcakes a ten, even the savory spinach one that everyone else spits out.

Before I know it, the sky is turning pink and orange, and the clouds are thickening like a storm's coming. Riley wants to walk us all home together, but I live in the opposite direction. "Bye!" I say, walking backwards down her driveway. "See you tomorrow!"

And then I jog through campus just to touch the stallion statue, and head around the tree-lined quad. I'm watching for Dexter and his soccer ball when I realize.

My notebook. I left it in Riley's room.

I start back, but the dark clouds cover the sunset and the light sprinkling turns to hard rain, soaking my clothes and making me shiver. The sky lights up with a stab of lightning and thunder rumbles past the mountains, wind rocking the trees. Mom will be worried.

So even though my heart feels not right and my skin is prickly, I convince myself it's going to be okay. Just one night without my SOPs. Riley will put my notebook in her super-secret safe hiding place. She'll bring it to school for me tomorrow. She knows the value of a lab notebook.

Just one night. I can handle it.

I duck into the rain and race home.

# TWENTY-FOUR

THE NEXT MORNING I tell Dad that Elizabeth can't come to the Snoozatarium.

"Oh?" he says over his coffee, which he's slurping while trying to put on his shoes.

"But I might have a new friend to bring, if that's okay?" It's something I thought about a lot last night after I got home.

It's like Mom has sonic hearing all of a sudden. "A new friend?" She pounds down the stairs, a mascara wand in one hand and her brush in the other.

"It's no big deal," I say.

"Why can't Elizabeth go? What happened?" Mom says.

My face burns. "Nothing."

"I always told you she was boring," Brooke says from the couch. "Called it!"

"Anyway." I hand Dad the bagged-up tambourine and soccer cleat plates because they were really stinking up my closet. The tambourine petri dish grew clusters of yellow dots with black middles, something I've never seen before. I took several pictures, a few zoomed-up really close, and wrote up some notes. MUSIC ROOM TAMBOURINE now has its own tab in the back of my microbiology binder.

"Wow," Dad says. "Let's put some of these under the microscope when you come to the lab today."

"Cool," I say. Maybe there's a new bacteria. Maybe we'll call it the Madeline Little.

When I go out to the bus stop, Mr. Sid's sitting on his front porch next to an overflowing basket of baby pumpkins, sipping from a steaming GARDENING IS FOR REAL MEN mug.

"Are you going to throw those little pumpkins at Bark?" I say.

"I wouldn't do that!" Mr. Sid puts his tea down. "I'm only going to throw them at my fence to make him *think* I'm trying to throw them at him."

I give Mr. Sid a long look. "Anyway, I'm going to the Snoozatarium for my birthday," I say, grinning and leaning over his fence. "I'm going to invite a new friend."

Mr. Sid strides over to his birdbath and dumps out the old water. "Fantastic, Maddie!"

"We'll get to sleep inside the planetarium at the science museum and have an astronaut breakfast the next morning."

"Sounds like a perfect way to celebrate a birthday. Going to be an exciting week for everyone." He looks out at his garden and plucks a weed out of a pot of herbs.

Brooke lumbers out of our house. "Ew, it's so cloudy out here," she grumbles.

The bus pulls up, loud and dirty, and I say goodbye to Mr. Sid and his peaceful garden. I climb the bus steps behind my sister and she gives me the evil eye, like I'm too close. She's all evil eyes and end of the world lately. I sit in the way back, as I do every day, and take out a bagged petri dish. It's the one from the swab of Riley's sister's retainer, and even after only one night, it's speckled with dots of bacteria. I can't wait to show Riley.

At school, I wait at her locker. When she doesn't come, a tingle of worry starts in my chest. What if she's not here with my notebook today? I shift my backpack and let the first bell ring before I run to homeroom, fear seizing my heart. What if she didn't even notice my notebook was still there? What if her mom accidentally throws it into the laundry with the sheets from Riley's bed? I breathe deeply. I should have gone back in the storm to get it. What's a little lightning when your science notebook is alone and unattended?

When I walk into Independent Study after homeroom, relief floods over me. They're all here, the entire lunch table crew: Riley, Katherine-with-a-K, Amy and her encyclopedias, Timothy Tangier, and a giant model T. rex, all standing around the table next to my usual seat.

"Hey, Riley." I stand next to her. "Did you bring my —"

She reaches into her backpack and tosses my notebook in my direction. The hard spine hits my wrist and my notebook flaps to the floor, landing open, splayed out so everyone can see my writing.

"Oh, sorry," she says. "Maybe you should write an SOP on how not to forget your notebook next time." For a minute she seems serious, but then everyone laughs, so I do too, grabbing my notebook from the floor and checking the pages for damage.

I sit at my table, eyeing Riley and the rest of the group, and start copying notes from the board as Amy squeezes in next to Katherine-with-a-K, Timothy, and his T. rex.

"Well, aren't we cozy today," Mrs. Blickman says as she walks into the room. "Amy, you don't want your usual seat?"

Amy shakes her head.

"I guess it's your lucky day, Madeline, with a whole table to yourself," Mrs. Blickman says, and a lump forms in my belly. "Today I'd like to hear a progress report from each of you on your projects. We have three more weeks until the paper is due, and I just want to make sure we're all on the right track." Mrs. Blickman eyes the dinosaur, the size of an overweight St. Bernard. "I see you are making good headway, Timothy."

My progress report is almost last, after Timothy's report on the archaeology dig in China, Amy's report on the inaccuracy of the Pluto entry in the *P* encyclopedia, and Katherine-with-a-K's spelling of the first twenty *W* words in the dictionary. Riley talks about real-life astronaut Dr. Leopold, and how she'll be interviewing him by video chat next week. I tell them about the autoclave and my deadly dry ice. I describe my lab bench, name plate, and lab coat. I even have an extra pair of goggles in my backpack, and I put them on. Somebody whispers "B-O-R-I-N-G."

A red-hot realization seeps into my chest.

When everyone leaves, I stay behind and open my notebook. I flip through all the pages. And at the end I see, written under my last observation, in ugly red ink:

*Introduction, Discussion, and Conclusion:*
*Madeline Little is the worst friend in the history of ever.*
They read my secret notebook.

# TWENTY-FIVE

I WANT TO BURN my lab notebook. Leave it in the middle of the street. Throw it off a bridge into the river. I never want to see it again. Ever in my life.

I think of all the observations I've recorded, all of my thoughts on middle school. There's an SOP about wearing too many clinky bracelets. And one about avoiding annoying people who spell everything instead of talking like normal human beings. There's even a discussion in there about how not to bang into people when you're carrying way too many encyclopedias.

At lunch, I get a bathroom pass and sit scrunched on top of a toilet with the lid closed. Girls with hairbrushes and fancy-flavored lip gloss keep banging into the bathroom, laughing too much and chattering about boys and boots. They talk about friends who aren't there, and my face burns. They knock on my stall door and pull on the handle, a line forming with one less toilet for so many girls. But I don't answer until a teacher comes. And it's okay because then lunch is over anyway and it's time for science.

I'm relieved when I don't see them in the halls or near my locker. I'm relieved when Timothy Tangier moves his seat to the corner of the art room even though that means he has to sit next to stinky Todd. I start to think maybe I will survive this terrible day if I just pretend that nothing is wrong and that I don't care. But then it's last period. Gym. And Riley is there.

We sit one in front of the other in our assigned squad positions, stretching before class starts. My brain is a flurry of panic. I have five minutes to say just the right thing to her, but I can't concentrate over the squeezing feeling in my body. The shame and sorry-feeling because Riley read the hurtful things I wrote. Me, her almost-friend.

But there is also a sting of anger, red and hot. Because the first rule of being a scientist is that you don't read someone else's notebook. You just don't. And maybe Riley's not the kind of scientist I thought.

And then the whistle blows and my five minutes are up.

Riley turns to me and says just one word: "Mean." She

says it close to my face, and I can smell her peppermint breath before she turns and runs to line up for a lacrosse stick.

The only thing I can think of is Grandpa and how he always said the most important thing in life is to be kind. Always kind.

It feels like everyone's looking at me, like they know what happened. They know I'll never make friends in middle school because I'm mean.

I don't line up for a lacrosse stick. I grab the bathroom pass instead and tell the teacher it's an emergency. And then I don't go to the bathroom in the locker room, or to the crowded bathroom by the cafeteria. I keep walking. Past the woodshop. Past the auditorium. Straight to the lesser-used bathroom by the closed library where Brooke cleaned me up after my bloody nose on the first day of school.

When I swing the door open, I find my own sister inspecting herself in the mirror. Abby is nowhere to be seen.

"What are you doing?" I ask. I know something is wrong. Brooke's pale and holding a wet paper towel on her elbow. "Are you okay?"

She shakes her head. "I'm fine, Madeline. Go back to your studying or whatever."

"Is that nasal spray?" I point to the bottle next to the sink. "My nasal spray?"

"Seriously, Maddie, go."

I can see my name on the prescription stickered to the side. She stole my nasal spray. "Brooke."

"Stop!" she yells, breathing hard. "I hit my arm in gym and that stuff is working for me."

A joint bleed. Even the slightest injury can mean internal bleeding for Brooke. It's just like when she banged her knee on the coffee table last year. Her entire knee got stiff and swollen. She had to go to the hospital for an infusion.

"But the doctor said my spray won't help you."

"They're wrong. I've been using it all this week. My allergies, you know? They're giving me more nosebleeds than usual. And the spray is working." She wobbles and I lunge to catch her. "Ow!" she squeals. "Don't touch my arm."

Her elbow is already swelling with blood and her body is full of the wrong medicine. "I'm calling Dad."

"No. Cheerleading pictures are today, and I'm not going to miss it." She reaches for the nasal spray. "I just need more of this, probably." And before I can pull the spray out of her hands, she gives herself another squirt.

"You can't use it that much!" I say. "You have to follow the procedures or it can be really dangerous."

Brooke cackles. "You and your procedures, Maddie. Not everything is a science experiment."

"You're sick. Don't be stupid, Brooke. You can miss cheerleading pictures." She's sweating and pale, and I list the symptoms of using the medicine wrong. "Do you have a headache? Dizziness? Diarrhea?"

"Ew. Seriously, what do you know about anything, Madeline?" Brooke stumbles, dabbing her elbow with the paper towel, as if she can stop the bleeding inside. "News flash — you're not a real scientist."

"Brooke —"

"That new friend of yours is imaginary, right?" She pinches my cheeks. "What do you know about anything if you can't even make a real friend? You should write an experiment on making friends. Like a friendship experiment."

"She is real," I say. "And I write SOPs, not experiments."

"Do you know why Grandpa wrote all those SOPs?" Brooke's voice is crackling with menace.

"Shut up." I put my hands over my ears. "Shut. Up."

"Because he had dementia, Madeline." She pokes me

in the chest. "You need to know it. He was demented. Losing it."

My body pulses with something hot and searing and ugly. "He was not."

She grabs on to the counter, unsteady. "He thought the microwave was a time machine, Maddie."

"He *pretended* it was a time machine," I say. "There's a big difference."

"Really? Is there really a difference?" Brooke stares at me, her eyes bloodshot, her skin ghost-white. "You know what? You're just like him."

"I'm not losing it," I say. "And neither was Grandpa." But I think about how I invited the autoclave to my birthday. *Pretended.*

"You talk to your Einstein poster," Brooke says, wetting more paper towels with cold water and draping them across her elbow, which is still swelling with blood.

I step away, pointing at her. "You're the one losing it. You know you're sick, but you just ignore everything so you can be in a picture?"

"You don't get it, Madeline," she says. "You act like you're so smart, but everyone knows the real truth." She gets right in my face, her breath sharp with sickness. "You're just a big failure.'"

I push her away. My heart is thumping. So much blood and fire and thumping, vibrating, pinching hatred. I open the door and it smacks me in the knee, but I barely feel it. I'm so out of here. "Don't call me for help!"

The door closes behind me and I hear her muffled, "I won't." And then I feel lost in the deserted halls. My blood feels too hot, like it's pooling inside my body, ready to burst. I find myself standing outside the school nurse's office. The door opens and out comes the nurse.

"You just going to stand there?" she says.

She leads me to the last open cot and sits me down, sticking a thermometer in my ear like Mom does.

"I'm not sick—"

"Well, you don't look too good. You sick on tacos, too? I warned those lunch ladies about too many spices." The nurse pulls up her stockings. "Nobody ever listens to the one who knows, though. You stay here."

"Nurse!" the kid next to me calls.

The nurse tosses me a thin blanket before she moves on. The other kid better not have lice. That's all I need. Nobody wants to be friends with a weird girl who lives her life according to an SOP. Add a bloodsucking insect parasite to the mix, and it will be just me and Einstein for the rest of my life.

I sit until the final bell rings. I wait until the surge of kids in the hallway comes and goes, and then I emerge, slow and silent. My body is numb and I walk carefully back to the gym for my backpack so I won't disturb the ugly words Brooke put in my head. I'm not a failure. Imaginative, maybe. Smart, brilliant, creative. Not a failure.

When I get on the bus, Brooke's not there. She must have gone to cheerleading, as she said she would, and I feel a wave of panic. As soon as I get home, I'm telling Mom and Dad everything. How she's been lying in her medical logbook and using the wrong medicine and keeping injuries a secret. They'll know what to do.

But then the bus stops in the school driveway, lined up behind all the other buses, because there's a siren and it's getting closer. An ambulance pulls in, lights flashing, medics jumping out as the back doors fling open. A gurney is pushed out and rushed into the school. The ambulance is blocking the buses and I try to close my eyes but I can still see the lights through my eyelids.

Then they're back, pushing the gurney carefully over the speed bumps, three medics working together. Kids are staring at me on the bus now and I try not to look out the window, afraid of what I'll see. But when I finally do, they're rolling the gurney back into the ambulance. And I see enough of it to know it's not a football player with a torn muscle or a lunch lady with a cut finger.

It's my sister.

# TWENTY-SIX

M R. SID MEETS ME when I get off the bus, Bark right behind him. "Got a call from your folks," he says, rubbing his neck. "Seems like Brooke—"

"I know. Do you know if she's going to be okay?" Which is a baby kind of question to ask, because adults always say yes even if they don't mean it.

"They think it's a reaction to medicine." We walk slowly to Mr. Sid's front yard, Bark following us, wagging and bouncing. "Your mom's gone to the hospital, and your dad will come meet you at home. I'm sure they'll know more soon."

I look over at my house. I know there's a key hanging in the overgrown bush, but I don't feel like being in an empty house right now.

I sit on the sidewalk against the fence, outside Mr. Sid's yard. "I'll just do my homework here, okay?" Bark climbs into my lap as soon as I take my backpack off.

"Okay. Are you sure? Do you need anything?" Mr. Sid bites his lip.

"I'm good." I take my lab notebook out like I'm getting down to work even though the sight of it makes me want to throw up.

Mr. Sid disappears inside, leaving me to sit against the fence. Just me and a snoring dog. I try to keep my brain blank because that feels like the only way to survive this unknowing; I watch the clouds and count the spots on Bark. But my mind keeps going back to Brooke's pale face in the bathroom, and me storming out and abandoning her there. Bark nuzzles closer, his head on my arm.

I hear the gate click, and see that Mr. Sid is back with a tray of cookies and two mugs of tea. He sits next to me and we sip the sweet, warm tea, and I pet Bark. We don't talk for a long time, until Mr. Sid points at a cloud.

"Look, a brontosaurus," he says. "And I don't mean apatosaurus. I mean brontosaurus." He bites into a cookie. "They made a mistake, and now scientists are saying both existed."

I'll have to consult with Timothy on this later. If he ever talks to me again.

"I believe you." I drink the rest of my tea, my belly

feeling better but my brain still buzzing with everything bad. I want to sleep through all of this like Bark. Just pretend today never happened.

When Dad finally pulls into our road, he drives right past me and stops in front of our house. He jumps out of the car. "I need Top Hat Panda!" he calls to me as he unlocks the front door. "Do you know where Top Hat Panda is?"

I race over. "Downstairs, in her room!" My backpack feels like it's full of bricks. Dad's already thundering down to the basement when I come into the house, dropping my backpack onto the couch.

"Where?" he calls.

"She keeps that one under her pillow!"

"Got it!" He runs back up the stairs, taking a breath at the top.

"Dad?" I'm terrified to ask anything. Is she okay? Did she tell them I left her? Can they make her stop bleeding?

"She's been using your nasal spray. Did you know that?"

My face flushes. "Yes. She told me today."

"Well, it's made her really sick." Dad grabs his keys and I follow him to the car. "She was using too much, and now her salt levels are dangerously low."

Dangerous. "Like how dangerous?"

Dad looks tired, with circles under his eyes and a shadow of a beard, like he hasn't shaved in a day or two. "She's getting the best care possible right now, Maddie. Don't you worry."

We park in the patient parking lot and walk in through the emergency room entrance.

"Go ahead to the lab. Tyrone's there, and he'll keep you busy. I'll see you up there in a little while, after Mom and I talk to the doctors," Dad says, and then heads in the other direction to give Brooke her panda.

He's halfway down the hall when he spins around and jogs back. "Love you," he says, kissing me on the forehead.

I wonder how much he'll love me when he finds out I'm the one who left Brooke when she needed me the most.

# TWENTY-SEVEN

TYRONE IS SIPPING coffee by the vending machines when I come into the lab area. "How's Brooke?"

"Fine, I guess. Maybe."

"I was just looking over your dad's first round of results with the new enzyme." He holds up his papers. "Looking good."

Tyrone probably never had any problems as a kid. I already know he had a lot of friends. Bet he also had a bunch of brothers, and they were all scientists and had a giant scientific collection in their backyard shed and went to a private school with a rocket launch pad in the parking lot or something. I bet nobody used the wrong medicine or had someone read their confidential science notebook when they weren't looking.

"Do you have any brothers?" I ask.

"Nope." He drops his papers on Dad's desk. "Only child."

Figures.

Like Dad said, I'll keep myself busy. Buttoning myself into my lab coat, I head for my bench. I put on my fuzzy gloves and load up my icebox with smoky dry ice. I blow on it and a cool puff of dry ice pours over the side. One more scoop to be safe, and then I open the freezer.

Sitting down in front of my little science tubes and canisters and racks, I push the horrors of the day out of my mind. I'm a scientist. A real microbiologist. In a college. About to make a discovery that will change everything. Because the reality of this disease is that it's ruthless and unpredictable. It doesn't just ruin silk shirts and first days of school; it lurks beneath the skin at all times. And sometimes it ruins whole lives.

How would our lives be different if I didn't have to worry about a nosebleed that might never stop? If Brooke didn't have to be wheeled out of school on team picture day, pale and weak and angry? If Grandma were still alive? What if one day we made the right kind of discovery, and then blood just stayed in the body like it's supposed to?

I pull out a new inventory sheet so I can do my part in this discovery process. So far I've inventoried three hundred thirty-four things: tons of frozen enzymes in tubes, samples dating back four and five years, an actual cow brain, and lots of tubes of blood. When I found the cow brain I didn't even feel like throwing up. That's how much of a scientist I am already.

An ear-piercing screech erupts from the autoclave room and I drop the tray of frozen tubes I'm holding. They skate across my bench, one or two landing on the floor.

"Do you mind checking on the autoclave?" Tyrone says, bent over into one of his cabinets.

"Sure." I collect the runaway tubes and return them to my ice bucket, then fast-walk to the autoclave room, blocking my ears. I punch the big red silencer button by his door, and he gives a quick beep in surrender and goes quiet. The read-out screen flashes CYCLE COMPLETE. I want to tell him to forget about the Snoozatarium. That I'm not going because I don't even have a single friend in this world. But it feels so peaceful and warm in his little back room that after I write in his logbook, I can only manage to pat his steel wall and leave.

I pull my gloves off and go back to the lab, where Tyrone is at the sink, washing glassware.

Dad strides into the lab. "Hey."

"How's Brooke?" Tyrone and I say at the same time.

Dad stands in front of my bench and straightens my handwritten nameplate. "She's got a pretty nasty joint bleed, and they're doing an infusion right now. But it's her salt levels they're most worried about."

"From using the nose spray?" I ask, and Dad nods. If only I had known it was so serious. If only I hadn't walked out on her.

"They're going to transfer her to the hematology center a few hours away once she's ready. Nana will stay with you while we get this all figured out," Dad tells me.

The guilt from the entire day wells in my throat like an oversize balloon.

Dad straightens. "Madeline. How did this get here?" He pulls a tube from behind my ice tray.

My stomach drops. A runaway I missed.

"Our enzyme." Dad's voice is getting deeper, the way it always does when he's upset. "Was this sitting out all this time?"

I grab the tube, no larger than one of my fingers. "It's still cold," I say, though it's far from frozen anymore.

Tyrone rushes over and takes the enzyme from me, holding it up to the light. "No, no, no."

"Still cold" isn't good enough. I feel like I might throw up. Dad curses. "We'll never get another one in time for the funding. I need these results." He moves into action. "Someone get ice!" I scoop more dry ice into my bucket. "No, wet ice!"

Wet ice? I spin around, looking.

"We can't let it refreeze," Dad says, pushing everything on my bench aside. My inventory sheet floats to the ground. Tyrone delivers a bucket of regular ice, sinking the tube of enzyme into the center of it, burying it in the coldness.

"Dad, I—"

"I thought I told you not to touch it," Dad snaps at me. "What was it doing out of the freezer in the first place?"

"It was in the rack with the things to be inventoried, Dad." But of course it's my fault. All the tubes look the same. Why didn't I check the labels first? "I didn't mean . . ."

"This is my fault. I probably put it in the wrong rack," Tyrone says.

"You need to pay attention when you're in the lab," Dad says, and I'm sure he's talking to me. "It's very temperature-sensitive." There's a redness creeping up his neck. "This is not good."

"Dad, what can I do?" But nobody hears me. He and Tyrone are doubled over the ice bucket like it's a sick baby. "Dad?"

I'm falling apart. I can feel it like a vibration in the Earth, moving up my legs, into my bones, out to my fingertips.

Dad's phone chimes and he pulls it out of his pocket. "Nana's here, Maddie. Go ahead home. I need some time to concentrate."

I bolt, tripping over the biohazard bin in the aisle, nearly toppling it and spilling its innards. I slow down at the door to the lab, moving carefully around the glass cylinders lined up on the tile floor, not wanting to wreck anything else. I think I hear my name, but when I hold my breath, the lab is quiet except for the autoclave's little chirp — I was only hoping I'd heard someone call me.

My lab coat still on, I'm running home as the sun disappears behind the mountains. When I hit Main Street, Grandpa's house is lit up by the setting sun. The stained-glass window in his attic glows. There is a U-Haul in the driveway, parked in the shadows, next to his car with the For Sale sign.

I can barely look at the truck; it's probably bursting with Grandpa's most treasured things. I close my eyes as I inch past it, crouching down to reach into the third light on the front walkway.

It's still there. My key.


With all of his things missing, Grandpa's house doesn't smell the same. I flick on every light switch I can find and wonder how long it would take me to unpack the U-Haul.

Put everything where it belongs. The U-shaped couch back in the living room, the mirror over the fireplace, and the HOME IS WHERE YOU LIGHT YOUR BUNSEN BURNER sign over the kitchen sink.

I feel like I'm getting bubonic plague again. But I manage to keep myself together as I climb the stairs. Turning on more lights, I open the door next to Grandpa's bedroom and take the steps into the attic.

Everything is gone, even his reading lamp and his puffy chair next to the window. The room smells like mustiness and fake lemons. I wish I had my jacket, because I'm shivering. My footsteps echo on the bare wood floor, and I tiptoe to the tiny little door in the wall.

I put my thumb over Grandpa's paint-splatter fingerprint on the doorknob and concentrate, trying to leave my terrible day at the door, and by some miracle, it actually works a little. I duck inside and the smell of paint is strong. Grandpa's art studio is just as I've always known it. His entire house has been packed and sold, but someone forgot about this little door in the attic. The most important one.

And I wonder if anyone will notice if I just sit in this tiny room forever.

# TWENTY-EIGHT

THROUGH THE WINDOW, I see that the sun is nearly gone now, and the street is all shadow. I turn on the lamp by the easel. Grandpa's painting of the Von Willebrand factor is still there, half-finished. I pick up a dry brush from the windowsill and pretend-paint the rest of the picture, adding the missing domains and connecting them to Grandpa's. In my head it looks beautiful, but I am no artist, so I put the brush down and sort through the finished canvases under the window.

They're mostly Grandma. Grandma in the sun, Grandma at the lake, Grandma holding a baby. In the bottom right-hand corner of every painting are two little *L*s for *Leonard Little*, smushed together and barely readable. I look back at the Von Willebrand factor, unfinished and unsigned and so different from the rest of his paintings. He must have wanted to show everyone that even though he wasn't allowed around chemicals anymore and needed

SOPs to tie his shoes, the scientist was still in there somewhere.

I know Grandpa had dementia. It's something that happens when you have Alzheimer's disease. But I wish everyone could just remember him as he used to be. Before he stopped remembering our names and started asking when Grandma was coming home from the store. He wrote SOPs to make sense of things, to keep things straight. Just like Von Willebrand is a disease of the blood, Alzheimer's is a disease of the brain.

I pull jars of fresh paint from the cabinet and line them up on the counter. There's a piece of paper taped to the wall. An SOP on how to mix the paints to get the color of Grandma's hair just right: two parts rosebud to one part sunray to three parts chestnut.

I pull more paints out until the entire counter is a jumble of jars, some nearly empty, some never opened. Paintbrushes, cloths, palettes, and empty canvases. I balance them all on the tiny counter space until Grandpa's paint cabinet is empty.

Von Willebrand is staring at me, half-finished and lopsided. I push the empty jars and broken paintbrushes from the counter into a box and put it by the door. And then I line up some colors, reds and pinks and oranges, using my finger to mix because it's not about procedures now. It's all about finishing what's been started. And I'm left with a shade that's orange lollipop, campfire, and sunset all mixed into one. I see the Von Willebrand in my mind and I paint the missing domains, my squiggles too loose and my lines too thick.

But it's finished. And I even add an *ML* for *Madeline Little*, smushed together at the bottom of my not-so-masterful masterpiece.

I lean against the windowsill as I wait for it to dry, wondering how long Grandpa's art room will stay his art room. And then I get tired, so I grab a pile of clean paint rags and use them as a pillow, stretching myself out under the easel. I watch the paint dry from a completely different angle.

There's a hard knock on the little attic door and I sit up, walloping my forehead on the easel. I must have fallen asleep. "Madeline?" someone calls. "Madeline, I know you're in there."

"Nana?" The box of paint jars is wedged between the door and the art table, keeping the door from opening more than a crack. I try to stand up but the easel has me trapped, and I have to be careful stepping through its legs so it doesn't topple over. My painting is still wet, some of the squiggles dripping down the canvas.

"You have everyone worried," Nana says, and I can hear her little dog, Mouse, snuffling at the door. "Come on out of there now. Something's blocking the door."

The bad dream that was my day rushes back to me like a pounding headache. I wipe my nose and see blood, pink and dainty. But before I can even grab some clean paint rags it drips onto the floor, thick and red and dangerous. "Just a minute!"

"Madeline." Dad's voice, rough and loud. "Madeline Avery Little, open this door."

"Hold on a sec." I grab more towels. Tiny dog claws scratch at the door.

"You picked quite a night to run away, Madeline." Dad pushes the door against the box, but it doesn't budge.

"I have a bloody nose," I say, and then there's silence.

"Open the door," Dad says, quieter.

Holding a wad of paint rags up to my nose, I pull the box out of the way and the door opens. "I need some paper towels."

"When did it start?" Dad says, all business.

"Just now."

"Where's your spray?"

Mouse shoots past us, smelling the canvases by the window.

"Brooke had it," I say.

Nana's hand is on my shoulder, squeezing. "Come on, Mouse." She whistles for the dog. "We'll get some more towels."

Dad's on his phone, which is perched in his neck so his hands are free to pinch my nose. "Found her," he says. "Dad's house. Okay. Love you. Bye."

When he hangs up, we don't say anything. Sometimes he looks at his watch. Sometimes he clears his throat. I picture Brooke in a hospital bed and wonder if in a few months I'll be there too. And what if someday they won't be able to stop the bleeding? What if the enzyme was the key to everything, and I ruined it?

"It's slowing down," Dad says, relaxing the pressure on my nose and reaching for some clean paint rags. "You're to carry your nose spray at all times now."

I dab a few more times and peek out the open door for Nana.

"Wow," Dad says, thumbing through the paintings by the window. "There are so many." He stands up, looking all around. "We forgot about this room. I actually had no idea he was still painting." He sees the SOP for Grandma's hair and takes it off the wall to read it.

"Same color as Brooke's hair, I think," I say. Dad shakes his head slowly.

I wonder if it's too soon to say sorry again. Grandpa

would say it's never too soon, but Grandpa's not here to see Dad's bent shoulders and frowning face. Not in my whole life have I seen Dad like this.

Mouse bursts in, followed by Nana with a handful of tissues. "Took me forever to find these." I shoo the dog from the open jar of paint on the floor and he bounces away from me.

"I've got to get back, Mary," Dad says to Nana.

"You're not coming home?" I say, because it's late, the night as dark as a black hole.

He's standing with his hands on his hips, taking in Grandpa's secret art studio. "Tyrone's still at the lab. We're not finished. Mom's at the hospital with Brooke. You go home with Nana."

Nana steers me out of the attic, reminding me that my birthday's coming up, the big one-two, and asking what I want for breakfast. Her dog runs circles around us.

"Can I help you?" I ask Dad.

"No, Maddie," he says. "I should have said no from the beginning. Kids just don't belong in the lab." It's like a soccer ball hitting me in the gut, knocking the wind out of me.

We walk in silence back down the stairs, turning off all the lights and leaving through the garage. Dad won't even accept Nana's offer of a ride back to the lab. He waves goodbye and I climb into the front seat and watch him disappear into the dark of campus. Mouse pounces on me, lying down in my lap and falling asleep. And I hate myself for letting Dad go back to the lab before I said anything more. Not an "I'm sorry." Not even an "I love you."

Nana hums her own quiet tune as we drive. Mouse is making little purr-snore noises like everything is right in the world, but my mind is thumping and ringing all sorts of alarms. I recite the periodic table in my mind, backwards and forward, over and over again.

# TWENTY-NINE

$B$ROOKE GETS MOVED to the bigger hospital a few hours away and Nana won't take me to visit her all weekend because somehow, as if things aren't bad enough, I catch something that resembles the Black Death. Along with everyone else — my ex–best friend, my almost-friends, my sister, and my dad — the universe hates me too.

"Good thing you got this now instead of next week-end," Nana says, placing a mug of warm milk and honey in front of me. "Nothing worse than getting sick on your birthday."

I'm bundled up in our fleeciest blankets on the couch, Mouse at my feet, and I can't stop thinking about Brooke. Grandpa always said we're lucky. That if we had been born a few decades earlier, our bleeding disorder could have been a death sentence, as it was for Grandma. But now it's so manageable, he said, especially with all the new research. How could he have been so wrong? And what if I wrecked the enzyme that could have led to a breakthrough? A breakthrough that could save my sister's life? Even my own?

"I remember when your momma was sick on her tenth birthday," Nana says. "Broke our hearts. Had to cancel a magician and the snow cone machine." She scoots Mouse over to sit down with her own mug of something warm and steamy. Probably her cinnamon tea, not that I can smell anything right now.

"Did she have a lot of friends coming?" I say.

"Sure she did. Your momma always had a lot of friends."

I burrow deeper and roll onto my side, Mouse repositioning himself on my legs.

I stay on my sickbed couch for days, missing school, watching shopping shows with Nana, wishing I could just stay here for the rest of middle school. Mom calls home from the hospital every day at lunchtime, and Nana talks to her on the patio while I stay on the couch. Dad stops home for a quick shower every once in a while before returning to the lab, out of breath and rambling. I pretend to sleep.

The Black Death starts leaving my body mid-week.

Dad comes home for a quick dinner, and half of me wants to stop pretend-sleeping to ask if Brooke's ever coming home again. But I can't manage to open my eyes.

"How's Maddie?" Dad says to Nana.

Nana slurps her tea. "Doing fine. Probably going back to school tomorrow."

There's no way I'm going back to school. I cough, loud and raspy, tossing Mouse right off me. I keep my eyes closed, knowing they're both looking, wondering if I'm well enough to return to real life. Well, I'm not. And maybe I never will be.

I feel lips on my forehead. Dad's. A kiss? "No fever." He's just checking my temperature.

"I heard Brooke was released today?" Nana whispers, and I pull the blankets away from my ears.

"Yes," Dad says, his voice heading away from me and into the kitchen. "She's much stronger. They'll get a hotel room and stay up there for a few more days, though. The doctors are going to teach her how to self-infuse, and talk about other treatment options."

"And how about your work?" Nana says, real low. "The research."

Dad microwaves something. Probably a soup cup, tomato, his favorite. "We're hoping our report can show enough of the story to keep the funding. It's hard juggling everything, but I'm trying to make it work." He sips his soup. And then the next thing I hear is the front door close behind him.

The next morning when I come downstairs, my sickbed is gone, Mouse snoozing in my spot without me. "I'm still sick, Nana. Weak."

She pats me on the back. "Since when have you ever wanted to take another day home from school? Didn't you have perfect attendance last year?"

"And the year before." Things are different now. "Nana, I can't go back to school yet."

"You certainly can. You are a strong and able person, Madeline. You can do it."

"How about you teach me about Mesopotamia and stuff? I should be here when Brooke gets back."

"Whenever I had a heavy heart, you know what my mom always said?"

"I don't have a heavy heart, Nana." If I'm being honest, it's my whole body, my brain, my arms, even my feet —and I wonder how all this happened. How could I let everything get so out of control? Not only does everyone at school hate me for the mean things I wrote in my notebook, but I walked away from Brooke when she needed me. And I ruined Dad's research.

I sit on the bottom step and pretend to tie my shoe, blinking fast, because I'm not going to cry now. Not in front of Nana, who's talking about heaviness and hearts.

Nana sits down next to me. "My mom used to tell me this: First, you pick a star, the brightest and strongest in the sky. Then you think of one or two things that are really worrying you. It could be anything. A test. A boy" — she waggles her eyebrows at me — "or something bigger. Then you ask the star to worry about those worries for you. Just for an hour or two, or maybe overnight. So you can have a break, because everyone needs a break once in a while, right?"

It's like an SOP. "I'll remember that when I have a heavy heart someday," I say, but really I'm saying her words over and over in my head so I don't forget. I run up the stairs and fish my notebook out from under my mattress, tearing out a blank page. And before I can forget this SOP on stars, I write it down. One last SOP. I put it under my pillow for safekeeping.

# Thirty

IN HOMEROOM I HIDE behind a book of astronomy. I don't look at anyone the entire morning. Not even when Logan pulls James's pants down outside history class. I want the opposite of friends. I want to move to Antarctica. Just me and my crinkly, creased Einstein poster.

I don't mean to, but I look over at my old lunch table when I walk into the cafeteria. They're laughing and eating Three Sisters cupcakes. Someone I don't know is sitting in my seat, and I somehow manage to find one someplace else. That's fine anyway. I hate laughing. And I hate cupcakes.

I write an SOP in my head on *How to Move to Antarctica.*

*Step 1. Learn how to build an igloo for one.*

*Step 2. Obtain a dog and sled.*

*Step 3. Research polar bear diets and avoid contact.*

I don't dare write it down.

In gym class I'm forced onto Riley's volleyball team.

For a second I wonder if I should try to talk to her. Maybe I can remind her that just the other day she showed me her super-secret family meteorite. And how can she be mad at me for writing down my observations and conclusions? And also, isn't she a scientist too, and doesn't she know you never read another scientist's notebook?

But then she gives me a mean face and nearly decapitates me with her volleyball serve. So that's it, then. We're not friends. Which is okay with me.

The next day at school is no better, and I even take myself to the nurse, feeling a relapse of the Black Death coming on. But the nurse says it's only dehydration and makes me drink a cup of warm water. I take my time sipping, coughing loudly in case the nurse will change her mind and let me go home. She doesn't.

When a kid comes into the office, holding his belly like he might throw up, I gulp the rest of my water down and head back to class. Someone plastered Pumpkin Tournament signs around the school, and I ignore them, knowing Brooke probably won't be there to get her jersey after all.

Nana's on the back patio making dryer balls when I get home. No Dad. No Brooke. No Mom. And the naked lady is missing from the wall. At least that's an improvement.

I grab an empty yarn and wool box out of the recycling and head for the basement dungeon bedroom. I toss panda after panda inside, and then take all of the clothes down from the drying rack, slinging them over the box of pandas. Nana spots me from the backyard as I round the corner to the stairway to the second floor. The patio door slides open, but I call, "Lots of homework!" before slamming my bedroom door upstairs.

Nana has written *One more day to Madeline's b-day!* and *Let's Party Science Style!* and *Celebrate!* in green chalk on my pink wall. I rub it out. There could be a thousand more days before my birthday. It doesn't matter.

I dump out the pandas, some of them squeaking as they hit the floor. And then I fill up the box with everything science-related. My crucible, my burned-out beaker, my graduated cylinders, my test tubes. I even pack up all my petri dishes and sterile swabs, pushing them down inside the box.

I look at my plates for the first time since everything happened. They're overgrown and stinky. The fur collar sample barely grew anything at all, and the retainer plate with antibacterial soap is completely empty, not even one colony of bacteria. The other plate, without the soap, is thick with yellow and white bacteria, and I think how it's so unfair that all these germs can just get erased from the planet with a touch of soap. Why does it have to be so hard to find the cure for what Brooke and I have?

There's a knock on my door. "It's Mom, honey. I'm home with Brooke."

I open my door just enough to block her view of my room. "You guys are back? Is Brooke okay? Is Dad home too?"

"Everyone is okay," Mom says. "She's made a good recovery, but it was a close one."

"What do you mean?" I ask, because "close one" could mean a thousand different things. Like close to death? Or close to staying in the hospital for another night? Don't people understand that I need to know these things?

"It just means Brooke needs to take better care of herself and take her symptoms seriously."

"I missed three days of school, Mom," I say.

"Oh, my poor girl," she says, pulling me into one of her bear hugs, rocking me back and forth. "I know, and you didn't even have your own mother to take care of you." She pulls away for a moment to look at my face. "You're still pale. You feeling okay?"

I nod, imagining those three days with Mom instead of Nana. Buckwheat and raw oats instead of cinnamon toast and hot canned soup. We would have wound dryer balls for all eternity, and I probably would have gone back to school a day or two earlier. Mom's staring at me and I'm worried she's going to mention my break-in at Grandpa's house, but instead she kisses me on the forehead. "It's nice that I never have to worry about you."

I stare at her, because if she's so in tune with the Earth and nature and spirits, how can she not feel that my piece of the world is completely disintegrating? Does she not know I ruined Dad's entire research project?

Mom doesn't seem to notice that I have all of Brooke's pandas, or that my drawers are flung open and emptied onto my bed. She doesn't ask why my Einstein poster is sitting crushed by a crucible in a box. So I relax and swallow my words and let her go back downstairs to her dryer balls so I can pack up my life and take it to the dungeon.

First I take my box of science outside and deposit it next to our trash cans. It's years of collecting and work. My petri dishes, Eppendorf tubes, swabs, and lab camera. Even my Einstein poster. When I look back I can see the very edge of my microbiology binder sticking up out of the box. It looks like Einstein is staring at me, disappointed. But I walk away.

I'm hauling my last armful of clothes down to the dungeon when Brooke steps into the house. She's been sitting on the back patio in the sun with Nana and Mouse. She's pale and blotchy, her hand black and blue with bruises from the IV. Her hair is limp on her shoulders, unbrushed and scraggled.

"Mom?" she says. "Nana found these bamboo friendship bracelets for Abby and me online for like two dollars and—" She sees the blank space above the fireplace. "Hallelujah! You took the naked lady down!"

Mom shakes her head. "Just temporarily. Nana had the great idea of lending it to Mr. Sid for his Pumpkin Fest garden tour." She frowns. "But don't worry, we'll get it back."

Brooke notices me with all my stuff. "What are you doing?"

I sidestep past them to the staircase downstairs and make it halfway to the laundry room before Brooke calls after me, "What's with all the laundry? Do not enter my room without permission."

I glare at her, nearly losing one of my sensible cardigans from the top of the pile.

"Hey, you wrote the room-entering SOP," she says, holding her hands up, standing over me at the top of the stairs.

"I'm moving into the laundry room." I'm careful as I step down the last few stairs and then heave my clothes onto the cot. I had pictured Brooke and me having this big sisterly *I'm sorry* session when she got home. Apparently that's not going to happen. Somehow I'm not feeling sorry for anything right now, anyway. Except for maybe myself.

"What did you do with my pandas?" she says.

"Upstairs. I moved you out. Congratulations, you get your own room."

"What about the spider crickets?" Brooke calls.

"Don't care," I say, closing the door. "I just want you to leave me alone."

And she does.

# THIRTY-ONE

I SIT DOWN on the bed and listen to the *thump-thump-thump* of the wool balls Mom has felted in the dryer. There's a flashlight on a shelf by my head and I pull it down, bringing an old paint roller crashing down with it. I jump up and stand completely still, flashlight in one hand, slipper in the other, ready to defend myself from alien-insect life forms. Half spider, half cricket, entirely out of this world.

I push the curtain aside and skim the flashlight beam over the piles of clutter against the walls. No spider crickets that I can see.

"Are you okay in there?" Mom knocks.

"Sure," I say, stuffing the flashlight under my pillow.

"Nice place," she says, and I hear her open the washing machine.

"Thanks." But it isn't. She and I both know that. "Is Dad home?"

"He'll be home for dinner," Mom says through my

sheet curtain. "Maybe we should try clearing out some of the stuff down here, huh?"

I lie back on my bed and look at the tools hanging from the wall. "Yeah."

Mom's at the dryer now and I can hear her dryer balls bouncing into the laundry basket.

"Hey, Mom? Can we get our money back on those Snoozatarium tickets?"

She looks into my tent bedroom. "What? Why?"

"I just don't feel like going. It's going to be too busy tomorrow with the Pumpkin Fest, and Dad probably doesn't even want to go anymore."

"Don't be ridiculous!" Mom laughs. "You've wanted to go to this for months!"

"Not really," I lie. "I heard it's pretty stupid and boring." I can barely even get the words out. *Boring.* Nothing the science museum ever does is boring.

"You know that's not true," Mom says. "Go with Dad, Maddie. They're going to have ice cream and free rocket ship rides on the simulator."

"It's not always about ice cream and rocket ship rides, Mom." I turn over, signaling that this conversation is over, but a second later, Mom's rubbing my back.

"I'm sorry about Elizabeth, Maddie," she says. What exactly did Brooke tell her?

"Nothing to be sorry about. I'd rather sleep in my own bed than in a dirty planetarium. End of story."

Mom's quiet for a moment, but then she lifts her basket of dryer balls. "How about I call the science museum and see if I can exchange the tickets for one of those private planetarium shows?" I shrug and sigh and try not to look too forlorn. "Maybe next weekend? I'll see if it's available."

"Sure," I say, letting the soft mattress take me in. "Maybe next weekend."

Mom loads another batch of balls into the dryer and pats me on the back on her way out.

I must have fallen asleep, because when I open my eyes, I'm sweating and the dryer has stopped. My flashlight bounces to the floor as I tear out of bed. What time is it?

When I rush up the stairs, Mom and Nana are filling the dishwasher. "Is Dad home?" I ask, feeling lightheaded.

"He ran up to take a shower. I didn't want to wake you up for dinner—"

And I'm already halfway up the stairs, leaping two at a time, hyperventilating by the time I reach the top. Time stops as I stand there, nerves fizzing. I'm supposed to be the gifted daughter, the one who's going to follow in his scientist footsteps, the one who gets his paramecium jokes. I need to talk to him so something feels right again.

Putting my ear to Mom and Dad's bedroom door, I listen. Nothing. I knock. Silence, except for my heart, which is about to pound out of my chest. I push the door open a crack. "Dad?"

He's laid out on his reading chair by the bay window, which gives a perfect view out to our yard and the campus beyond. He's snoring, his briefcase propped up against the chair and his orange and green tie loosened. I tiptoe over and pull his glasses off, folding them and putting them on his briefcase.

"Sorry, Dad," I whisper. "Like, really, really sorry." I stand there for a good minute, and when he doesn't move at all, I walk back out of the room. The heavy ball of regret in my belly grows bigger.

Nana's waiting for me downstairs, a plate of meatballs in mushroom gravy at my place at the table. "Eat," she says.

I stab a meatball with my fork and leave it there. "I'm not hungry."

"I made it," Nana whispers. "One hundred percent meat."

"There's some tofu left on the stove if you want it,"

Mom says, coming up the basement stairs with a full basket.

I take a test bite of my meatball, surprised that it's warm and tasty.

"I made pumpkin turnovers, too," Nana says. "For my birthday girl."

I perk up, arching my neck to see the turnovers. And they're there, in all their pumpkiny goodness, on a plate next to Mom's box of buckwheat. "Thank you, Nana!"

"Mom," Brooke moans from the couch, my old sickbed, Mouse the traitor snuggled at her feet. "Please, Mom. Pleeeeeease."

"You're not going. Absolutely not." Mom puts her basket down on the coffee table, and I look at Nana, who looks back at me. I know what Brooke is moaning about. The Pumpkin Tournament.

Brooke pops up from the couch, and I flinch because she doesn't look like herself. Hair a mess, no makeup. Gray circles under her eyes. "Okay, forget about the afterparty at Pizza Palace. I'll just go to the game. I'll sit in the bleachers. I won't even cheer. I just have to be there."

"Have you looked in the mirror?" I say, and when I see the look on her face, I regret it. "I mean —"

"Shut up!" she squeals, looking like she'd hurdle the couch and tackle me if she could.

"You aren't ready to go out yet," Mom says. "Nana's going to keep you company here tomorrow."

Nana and I exchange another glance. Brooke's not going to be an easy patient.

"There will be another soccer tournament next year," Mom says, inspecting her dryer balls.

"There won't," Brooke says, digging back under her covers. And actually, she's right. She's in eighth grade — this is her last Pumpkin Tournament. Her only chance to get a jersey from a boy.

I take a tiny bite of a meatball. "I'm sorry, Brooke. Sorry you can't go."

"Shut up, loser." It's muffled from under her layers of blankets, but I still hear her. *Loser.* She's never called me that before. *Nerd, dummy, weirdo* — a million times. But never *loser.*

Nana stands up from the table, the ice cubes in her water glass clinking like it's summer on her back porch. Mouse bounces after her and I wish I could go back in time, to when all it took was a good pencil and my lab notebook to solve my problems.

# THIRTY-TWO

EVERYONE HEADS off to bed, Nana to her little makeshift guest room in the alcove on the second floor and Brooke to our old room, moving slowly up the stairs. Mom, busy counting her dryer balls, almost forgets to say good night. Seventy-three. A record. I have to admit, they look kind of pretty all piled up in every different color, felted to a perfect fuzzy softness.

Mom kisses me on the cheek. "Don't burn the house down, and also don't stay up too late. We all have big days tomorrow. Dad and I need to leave really early to get set up."

"I know how to work a toaster oven, Mom," I say, watching the pumpkin turnover brown, the icing getting melty. "I'll be twelve in three hours." I check my watch. "Actually, two and a half."

She yawns, patting me on the head. "Guess you're growing up." And then she heads up the stairs, Mouse bouncing after her.

I take a long time to eat my pumpkin turnover, avoiding my basement dungeon, though my body is feeling heavy and I'm trying not to yawn. Maybe I'll stay up all night, watch the clock as it turns midnight, and wish myself a proper happy birthday. The big one-two.

Eventually, I can't resist sleep any longer, so I head downstairs. I take each step to the basement slowly, looking, watching, waiting for something to spring out at me.

I check under my covers with a flashlight. Thoroughly. And then I climb all the way in and snuggle under the blankets. All is quiet.

It's hard to sleep with the fluorescent lights on plus a night-light plus a flashlight under my pillow for fast retrieval. It's also hard to sleep when all I see are mad, hateful faces when I close my eyes. Especially when I'm pretty sure I deserve them.

I see movement and whip out my flashlight, shining it into a shadow by the washing machine. There are three black things on the floor, and I just know they're spider crickets. Half spider, half cricket. All terrifying.

I leap out of bed, the spider crickets hopping at my feet, hitting me in the legs as I run for the door and swing it open to safety. How did I never know of this horror? Is Brooke that much braver than I am?

Upstairs the house is dark and the microwave says it's

close to midnight. *Happy birthday to me*, I think, pitching myself onto the couch. Brooke took all the blankets upstairs, but I don't care. I curl up, turn the TV on low, and fall asleep watching two guys selling protein shakes from Thailand.

When I wake up, the house is quiet and bright with early morning. Mom's basket of dryer balls is missing, and when I stand up, I see a giant HAPPY BIRTHDAY banner hung over the kitchen counter and a ton of balloons scattered on the floor. Mom must have gotten up really early to blow them all up. When I look outside, a car is missing from the driveway. Mom and Dad have already left to go set up.

I stand in the kitchen, picturing what it would be like to have a birthday party extravaganza like Brooke always does. Elizabeth would come with her telescope and a ton of green jelly beans. We'd all *ooh* and *ahh* over Riley's really real meteorite and Katherine-with-a-K would spell it for us whether or not we wanted her to. And then Amy would look it up in the encyclopedia of her mind and we'd all talk about our own scientific collections. We might even invite Timothy. That would be my perfect birthday party.

I sit in front of the TV. When I hear someone padding down the stairs, I'm surprised to see that it's Brooke who's up so early. My instinct is to flee to the basement. She's the last person I want to see while I'm sitting on the couch watching two ladies sell measuring cups on TV. On my birthday. Definitely what a loser would do.

"Morning," Brooke says.

I burrow into the couch. I watch the ladies flatten the measuring cups into little paddles. They're collapsible. Why didn't I ever think of that? I could have quit middle school to be a millionaire genius inventor. Who doesn't want collapsible measuring cups?

I hear a *fizzzz! pop!* and smell something burning, then look over the back of the couch to find my sister coming at me with a plate of turnovers stuck with three sparklers. *"Happy birthday to you . . . you smell like a zoo . . ."* she sings.

I stand up. "That's for me?" It's all I say even though there are a million words floating in my head. Like *Sorry.* Or *You're not the worst sister.* And *You're right about the spider crickets at night.*

We let the sparklers die out, batting sparks away from the magazines on the table, and then each take a turnover. But somehow, I just can't take a bite.

"Thanks for cleaning out all your science stuff upstairs," Brooke says. "It doesn't even smell like zombie poop up there."

I laugh a little, but mostly there is a giant ache in my chest as I picture all my treasures in the trash.

"You're not a loser," Brooke says, her mouth full. "I didn't mean to say that last night. I was mad."

I think it's an apology. I should accept it and say sorry too. I frown. "Grandpa wasn't losing it, you know. Like you said in the bathroom." I pick at the icing on my turnover. "He had Alzheimer's."

Brooke takes another bite, wiping her face with her arm. "I know."

"It's a disease." I pull layers off my turnover. "A really terrible disease." Worse than the plague. Sometimes maybe worse than Von Willebrand.

"I shouldn't have said that." She takes a bite and looks at me sideways. "You're not the only one who misses him."

We watch the measuring cup geniuses for a minute, who are now advertising collapsible strainers and bowls.

"Brooke?" I say, putting my half-picked-apart turnover on the coffee table. "I should never have left you in the bathroom at school."

"I wanted you to," Brooke says.

"I knew you were sick." I bite my fingernail even though it's already down to a nub from all the biting I've done lately. "Really sick." I can't believe that I can be the kind of person who would leave her own sister to suffer alone. It's like I don't even know myself anymore.

The measuring cup ladies are waving their goodbyes on TV, taking their brilliant inventions along with them.

"In a million years you never would have left me," I say.

Brooke eats the last bite of her turnover and wipes her hands on a napkin. "I'll forgive you if you forgive me."

I picture Riley with her aproned, bossy cupcake sisters, and for once I feel lucky Brooke is mine. "It's a deal."

# Thirty-Three

AFTER NANA comes downstairs, she and Brooke sing "Happy Birthday," Mouse barking and spinning in place. Mom calls from her dryer ball booth, and she and Dad sing over the speaker phone. We can barely hear them over the sounds of the Pumpkin Fest being set up, with all the hammering and testing of microphones and early-bird shoppers asking Mom questions. They promise that after all the dryer balls sell we'll have a family party at home with cake and presents and astronaut ice cream.

When they hang up, Nana puts an arm around my shoulder. "Now go get dressed. You have some business to do at the Pumpkin Fest."

"What? Me? What kind of business?" I heard the lunch table group talking about how they were all going to the Pumpkin Fest to win goldfish at the penny-toss booth and name them after constellations in honor of Astronomy Day. There's no way I'm going near them on my birthday.

Nana steers me toward my basement bedroom. "You know what I'm talking about."

As Brooke and I had finished our turnovers on the couch, I'd told her the secret about the lab notebook mishap, and why I couldn't find anyone to come to the Snoozatarium with me. Now I glare at her.

"What?" Brooke says, filing her nails at the table. "Nana's right."

I go downstairs and get dressed, thinking, *Shouldn't I get to choose what I do on my very own birthday? If having friends is this hard, then do I really want any?* I open my door and look up the stairs. Nana's standing there. She may look all warm sugar cookies, but when's she's made up her mind about something, she's a rock.

When I mope back up the stairs, she pulls me into one of her signature hugs. "First thing about growing up," she whispers, "is that when you do something wrong, you always make it right."

She sounds like Grandpa. I squeeze her tighter.

"Even the biggest messes can be fixed with a simple 'I'm sorry,'" she says. "And the scarier it feels to say it, the more it needs to be said."

I think of running out of the library, Elizabeth and Grace standing there, watching me. I picture Riley's mean face. "They don't even want to talk to me."

"That's why you do the talking. Show them they're important to you. Say sorry, and let it sink into their brains. Give the warmth of the words time to hit their hearts."

When I break away from Nana, I find Brooke at the table with Top Hat Panda, bottles and tubing and syringes laid out in front of her.

"My infusion kit," she says. From now on Brooke will self-infuse when she has a bleed. I take a breath because that means she'll be injecting herself with her own medicine. She shows me the tiny needle.

"Do you have to stick yourself with that?" I say.

She nods. "Right here." She points to a vein in her hand. "I did it already in the doctor's office. It's not so bad."

"You're braver than I am." I watch as she practices on Top Hat Panda, pushing fake medicine through a syringe connected to a skinny tube leading to the little needle against his plush paw.

"You'd be brave enough if you had to be," Brooke says.

And then Brooke gets special permission from Nana to walk me outside. We wrap up one of Nana's pumpkin turnovers and pay a quick visit to Mr. Sid.

"Breakfast," I say, dangling it over the fence.

Mr. Sid is pacing the porch, checking his watch, sitting down, then standing up again.

"You need to eat," I say, tossing him the turnover—which is a big risk, but he manages to catch it.

"And relax," Brooke says. "There's still half an hour before the garden tours start."

"You're going to win, Mr. Sid." His garden is a burst of color on our little street.

"Come over later for a crepe and hot chocolate. I'll be serving them all day." He sits down on a garden stool and takes a deep breath. "The painting really makes it, you know. Your Nana is a savior."

We admire the nearly naked lady propped on an easel among the flowers, happy she's no longer in our house, and then say goodbye and good luck to the sweating Mr. Sid.

"Like I was saying," Brooke says to me, her hand on her hip, "don't you know the first rule of friendship is to never, ever badmouth your friends in your diary?" Brooke's slowly morphing back into her old bossy self.

"It wasn't a diary," I say. "It was my lab notebook."

"And if you absolutely *have* to write about your best friend in your diary, you write it in code. Don't you know about codes?"

I roll my eyes.

"Okay, Brooke!" Nana calls. "I want you and your platelets back in this house, missy!" She's in her fuzzy bathrobe, Mouse in her hands, standing on our front porch. Brooke waves me a goodbye, fast-walking back to our house.

"I'll bring you back some apple cider!" I call. Once she's inside, I take a right, away from the Pumpkin Fest — because there's something I need to do first.

# Thirty-four

WHEN I GET to the lab, it's dark and quiet except for the whirring and ticking of the sleeping machines. I stop at my lab bench to grab my goggles from the top drawer. My stomach cramps at the sight of the ice bucket sitting there empty, but I put on my goggles and head down the hall to the only friend I have. I pull on a guest lab coat and enter the autoclave's room.

I flip a light on at the desk and sit in the rolling chair. Even the autoclave is still and cold. It's like the lab knows it's Saturday morning. "No birthday party today," I say. "Maybe next week."

Opening my notebook, I start to tear. I tear out each and every sheet. All of my SOPs on how to survive middle school: *How to Make a Friend on a Bus. How to Avoid Unwanted Interaction. How to Wear a Wrap-Around Sweater. How to Get Out of a Cupcake Tasting Party.*

Because how can you live your life by an SOP when there are so many variables? Brooke is right: There's no such thing as a friendship experiment. Or a middle school experiment. There's no formula. Life is too unpredictable, too complicated.

I stand over the biohazard bin next to the autoclave; it's filled with dirty gloves and pipette tips and empty buffer bottles. Snapping on a pair of gloves and plugging my nose, I stuff my SOPs and the remnants of my lab notebook down into the very bottom of the bin. On Wednesday the biohazard guys will come, like they always do. And then my SOPs will get incinerated along with the rest of the hazardous waste.

The lights go on in the main lab, shining under the door and pouring through the window above the door frame. I shouldn't be here. I sweep the leftover torn paper off the desk into a trash can and collect my things like the place is on fire. I try to dive under the desk, probably the worst place for someone to hide. How did I ever think I could be a genius scientist?

And then the autoclave buzzer goes off, pulsating and angry, and before I can reach the silent button, the door to the autoclave room swings open and my dad bustles in. He sees me and yelps, jumping back.

"It's just me!" I shout over the racket.

"What are you doing in here?" He rushes over to the

silence button, and with one push, he quiets the auto-clave. I glare at the machine.

Dad is staring at me, his arms crossed. He's so good at heavy silences.

I think, *Maybe the autoclave wants it this way. Maybe he's giving me my chance to speak up.* "I'm sorry, Dad. I'm sorry about the enzyme. Sorry I ruined your research." My words are all jumbled together. "Sorry I sneaked into Grandpa's house."

Dad's shaking his head, looking at the quiet autoclave. "Do you know how long we looked for you that night?" His hands are on his hips now; he's getting revved up. "Brooke was just admitted into the hospital, my entire research project was in crisis, and you go off and disappear?"

I'm surprised anyone looked for me at all. "Sorry," I say. "Just. Sorry."

Dad sits in his chair, plopping his lab notebook on the desk, and I wonder if I should leave. I stand there for a minute in the silent room, Dad staring at the wall. Nothing to say to me.

Right. I turn and head for the door.

Dad stands. Pulls me by my elbow into a hug. I can't help it. I start sobbing into his lab coat. Dad squeezes harder.

"I didn't run away," I splutter. "I only just —"

"I know," Dad says. "I know."

I'm trying to pull myself together, but it's like everything is pouring out of me. "I thought she was going to die, Dad."

"Oh, honey. Brooke was never going to die. She was very sick, yes, but her — your — doctors are amazing." Dad leans his chin on the top of my head.

"Do you think, I mean, what if —" I can't find the right words. "What if one time the bleeding never stops? For Brooke or for me? Like Grandma."

Dad leans back, looking at me. "They didn't know Grandma was sick, Maddie. Medicine is so different now. If she lived now, they probably could have saved her."

The autoclave chirps behind us and Dad peels away from me, wiping my face with the rough sleeve of his lab coat, and then strides across the room to check his readout screen. "Just like anything else, you have to watch and pay attention. Take all of your symptoms seriously. Start a medical diary."

I snort, because there is no way I'm keeping a diary of any kind anytime soon.

"Brooke ignored things," Dad says. "She didn't tell Mom and me enough, and we weren't paying close enough attention. And she took too much medicine. She could have avoided the hospital altogether."

I rock back on my feet, watching Dad type something into the autoclave's computer. "How's he doing?" I ask, nodding at the beast.

"The autoclave?" Dad says, and then he whispers, "Don't tell him, but we've called a service guy."

I almost smile, but instead I stare at the tile floor. "Dad? I ruined your enzyme." I look everywhere but at his face. At the floor. Ceiling. Autoclave. "What are you going to do?"

"Mistakes happen, Maddie. And it's not all your fault. The enzyme was in the wrong place to begin with." Dad sits on the desk. "Tyrone and I did as many experiments as we could before the enzyme started to deteriorate. We worked for almost twenty-four hours straight. It felt like grad school." He laughs and then gets serious again. "It would be nice if we had more data points for the report, but, well, this isn't the first time something hasn't worked out as well as I'd hoped."

I nod, my mind still a storm of regret. "That means no cure?"

"Maddie, the cure for Von Willebrand disease might never be found." Dad takes his lab goggles off and puts them in the desk drawer. "Our research is going to help patients living with the disease. Make it easier to diagnose and to treat. Help people live better lives. Sometimes that's just as important as a cure."

"But maybe you'll find a cure along the way?"

"There is always that possibility." Dad hops off the desk. "Sometimes during your research you stumble upon something you least expect."

And I know he's right. Maybe science can be a little bit unpredictable, like real life, after all.

"Happy birthday, by the way. No Snoozatarium tonight, though, huh?"

"Nope." I picture Elizabeth getting her sleeping bag in order, coordinating her pajamas with Grace's, trying to decide if there's room in her bag for her solar system slippers with real flashing lights and sound effects.

"Then we'll just have to celebrate at home." He kisses me on the forehead and starts out of the autoclave room.

And I follow him, without my notebook, and don't even look back.

# Thirty-five

LEAVE DAD at the lab so he can check on his samples and walk the three blocks to the Pumpkin Fest, feeling lighter. Scents of apple cider and hot dogs fill the air and the ground vibrates from the live music. I stop on top of the hill and watch the festivities below, looking for my mom. It doesn't take long to find the giant rotating Earth on Mom's booth, with her banner proclaiming, SAVING THE ENVIRONMENT ONE DRYER BALL AT A TIME!

I stop partway down the hill when I spot the lunch table kids. They're huddled over the duck pond game, fishing for prizes, laughing.

Dread crawls into my chest and I feel like I'm a thousand-pound boulder stuck in the hillside. I sit down at the base of a tree and ache to write in my notebook. I gave it up too soon.

Someone taps me on the head, and when I turn I find Dexter hopping around, juggling his soccer ball with his feet.

"I need a goalie. Come on," he says.

"I can't play goalie. Sports aren't my thing, and also I'm at the Pumpkin Fest right now."

Dexter looks around. "You mean that Pumpkin Fest?" He points to the bottom of the hill. "Looks like you're sitting up here by yourself without anything to do. I need a goalie — come on."

There is no way this boulder is moving from her hillside.

"You owe me. Let's go," he says.

"Owe you?" Do I need to remind him he almost broke my nose?

"Coach made me pay for that bloody shirt." He spins the ball in his hands, shaking his head. He taps me with a foot. "Come on. I need to try out my secret move before the tournament today."

He isn't going to leave the boulder alone. I take another look at the lunch table kids as they're collecting their duck pond winnings and moving on to the next game.

The small field where little kids play their soccer games is empty except for some fluorescent cones and a few abandoned water bottles. There are no regular soccer matches during Pumpkin Fest; just the big soccer tournament at the university fields later today. Basically, the whole middle school goes. And during halftime, the cheerleaders do a choreographed routine they've been practicing since before school even started. I've never told Brooke, but actually, it's pretty amazing. And for those five or ten minutes, the middle school cheerleaders are ce- lebrities.

Dexter picks up two of the cones and places them in the center of the field. "Stand between the cones, please. Don't let the ball in."

I so wish Brooke could go. I wish so hard, my head pounds. Dexter clears his throat impatiently. "Before dark, Maddie."

I trudge out to the cones and stand there. When he dribbles closer and lines the ball up to kick it right at me, I duck and cover myself with my hands. Dexter starts laughing.

"You're going to hit me!" I say.

As soon as I straighten, he does hit me, kicking the ball directly into my arm. "Ow!"

He's still laughing. "Did that really hurt? Come on. Don't be such a baby."

"It's actually my birthday today, thank you very much," I say. "I'm practically a teenager."

"Then don't duck when you see the ball coming,

birthday girl. Hit it out of the goal. Pretend the galaxy depends on it."

Now he's speaking my language. When the ball comes again, I bat it out of the way with my hand. And it doesn't hurt. I hit every ball out, even a super-low-and-to-the-right ball that I have to dive for. Actually, maybe I'm kind of good at this.

Dexter claps. "Okay, now for my new secret move." He does some fancy motions with his feet and makes like he's about to kick the ball to my right, but then he falls over the ball and drives it into the left side of the goal. The ball whizzes past me.

"Wow," I say.

"I know," he says.

"I really thought you just fell."

"I've been practicing for like two weeks," he says. "I call it the psych-out."

"Good job." But then I see bright red dribbling from his nose. "Wait, you're bleeding!" I whirl around, looking for paper towels and ice that I know are not there.

"Don't freak out," Dexter says, pulling his shirt up to his nose and sitting on the sideline. "I came down too hard and banged my nose. No big deal. I'm not like you guys."

"What?" I say, my face hot. Brooke once told me some

of the guys say things, even though she's always tried to hide the truth. Like not-so-nice things. And once, in sixth grade, a boy refused to hold her hand during the square dance unit in gym because he didn't want to catch her disease.

Dexter waves a hand. "No, I just mean I don't have a bleeding disorder."

"You know about that?"

"Mostly everyone knows." Dexter pulls his shirt away, and he's right — there's barely any blood. I sit down and we're quiet for a moment, me picking at a blade of grass and Dexter juggling the ball in his hand.

"Brooke just got out of the hospital, you know," I say. "She was really sick this time. She can't go to the tournament tonight."

"She's not coming?" Dexter says, his face flushing. "I didn't know she was that sick."

"She can't go to the Pizza Palace party either."

"Bummer," Dexter says, and then, after a minute, he takes a deep breath. "Can I tell you a secret? I was going to give Brooke my jersey. You know, like a friendship, like just because it was —"

"She would have loved that," I say, my heart thumping out of rhythm for a second. It's just unfair. All of this. She should be here. "Can't you give it to her at school or some-thing?"

Dexter shakes his head. "It has to be that night, and the whole team has to be there. It's tradition."

"What about the after-party? Is that a tradition too?"

"Not really," Dexter says. "I guess it's just a fun thing we do after a big game." He stands up, brushing grass and dry leaves off his shirt.

"Wait." I jump up. There must be a way to fix this. "I have an idea." I tell him what I'm thinking, just blurt the idea, and realize it's kind of half-brained.

Dexter juggles his soccer ball between his hands again. "You'd really want to do that for Brooke? Are you sure?"

I nod.

"There's one condition," he says, holding up a finger like I don't know what *one* means. "Go out for soccer."

"What? No! Absolutely no way." Has he not seen my lack of soccer skills every other day before today? "For-get it."

He smirks. "There's an indoor girls' league starting. They need a goalie." He drops the ball and holds my shoul-ders. "Just goalie. You're pretty good."

I groan.

"I'll talk to the guys tonight," he says. "But you have to try out."

"Fine. I'll make a fool of myself and try out. Happy now?"

He smiles. "Yes. Yes, I am." He picks up his ball. "I'll let you know what the guys say."

And then he jogs off the field with a wave and I head in the other direction, back to the Pumpkin Fest.

# Thirty-Six

WHEN I REACH the top of the hill again, I hesitate. I take a step. But then I hear Elizabeth call my name from behind me.

I don't even know what to say to her. All of this is my fault. Everyone is right; I don't know how to be a friend.

"I want to go to the Snoozatarium with you," Elizabeth says. "Mom said I could."

I shake my head. "No. You have to go with your school. It's okay. You have to."

"But it's your birthday."

"I made a mistake," I say. "I freaked out. I'm really sorry."

We just stand there for a minute, staring out over the festival. I don't see Riley or Katherine-with-a-K or Amy or Timothy anymore.

"I just want us to be friends again," Elizabeth says, sitting on the hill.

"Me too." I sit down next to her and pick up a stick,

drawing circles in the dirt. "I thought you wouldn't want to be my best friend anymore. That you'd like Grace more."

"That's not true." Elizabeth has her own stick and is drawing a star next to one of my circles. "Grace is okay. But you know, she picks her nose sometimes, and we know how unsanitary that is." She laughs, but I can't stop being serious right now.

"You're right about me not being the easiest to get along with," I say. "I don't have anyone to take that other ticket. And it's definitely my fault."

"I wish I never said that." She punches me in the shoulder. "You're super fun. I just meant —"

"No, really. This is the kind of stuff your best friend should tell you," I say. "We've only been in school for like a month and I've pretty much managed to get everyone to hate me. I should have listened to you." We draw more circles and stars in the dirt until we have our own galaxy.

"If it makes you feel any better, nobody at my new school really gets it when I show them my pencil collection. They think it's a little weird."

"They just have to get to know you better." I sniff and massage my arm where the soccer ball hit me. "Grace doesn't really pick her nose, does she?"

Elizabeth laughs. "Yes, she actually does. Sometimes."

I add a really badly drawn rocket ship. "Well, you're the one who said no one's perfect."

"Yeah," she says. "I'm learning to overlook it." She smiles at me in a worried kind of way. "I don't have much time. I basically just came to say happy birthday." She hands me a long skinny present that I can tell is a pencil.

"You wrapped this?" Never in all of our years of friendship have we wrapped gifts for each other. Wrapping is impractical and wasteful.

"I also have about five pounds of green jelly beans for you," Elizabeth says.

My gift is wrapped so tight, I pull the paper off in shreds. But it's not a pencil at all. It's a pen, with a purple top and shooting stars printed all over it.

"You got me a pen?" I say. "The queen of pencils got me a pen?"

"I saw you drop your friendship pencil at the library," Elizabeth says. "You didn't go back to pick it up." She picks up a leaf, twirling it between her fingers. "Anyway, I figured it was time for something more permanent."

I knock into her with my shoulder. "It's perfect."

Elizabeth has only a few minutes left before she needs to pack for the Snoozatarium, so I quickly tell her about Brooke and the nosebleeds and my lab notebook debacle. She tells me she learned how to make astronaut ice cream at school and promises to show me how. And then she's off, waving and running home.

When I glance down the hill at the festivities, I see the lunch table kids heading over to the dog rescue booth. Nana was right. I have some work to do.

# Thirty-seven

I WALK PAST the duck pond game, around the snow cone booth, and directly toward them. But once I'm close, it's like I'm paralyzed.

They're leaned over the puppy pen, laughing as the puppies lick and nibble and yip at them. Riley's not wearing a million clinky bracelets for the first time ever. Is it because of what I wrote? I'm standing there, a frozen statue of shame, when Katherine-with-a-K looks up and says "M-A-D-E-L-I-N-E!" The rest of them stand up. Riley crosses her arms over her chest.

I don't know what to do. You're supposed to run away from an angry mob, right? They look at one another and make some telepathic group decision to walk away.

"Wait!" I say, running after them. "Wait."

They stop. Behind them, the puppies are all yapping and whining, trying to climb out of the pen. "I'm sorry," I say to their backs. "I'm really, really sorry. Please."

Riley swirls around. "Like, sorry that you'd rather lie and tell me you can't come to my party because your Hungarian great-aunt was visiting and is allergic to cupcakes?"

"Or that you have an infectious skin disease that causes blindness and that is why you can't sit with me at lunch?" Katherine says, a hand on her chest. "That hurts, you know."

Amy points at me. "You have a serious issue, Madeline Little."

"Do you even have a Hungarian great-aunt?" Timothy Tangier says.

I sit down next to the puppy pen. One of the puppies nips my finger and I pull away. "I should have never written those SOPs. They don't really help you figure out middle school."

"No K-I-D-D-I-N-G."

Katherine is looking up into the sky, frowning, and Amy stares at the ground. Timothy cleans his glasses and keeps looking over at Riley. She's just standing there, staring at me, her arms still crossed tightly over her chest.

I ruffle a black puppy's ears, not daring to look anyone in the eye. "I was wrong. I wish I never wrote those things." No one says anything. I'm practically begging them to forgive me, and I'm just getting back mean, stony faces. What did Grandpa do when a sorry wasn't enough?

I stand up. "I can make you guys some cookies?"

Katherine-with-a-K, Timothy, and Amy look at one another, rolling their eyes.

"Let's G-O, guys," Katherine says, and the three of them turn their backs on me and take off. I think of what Nana said and hope she's right, that my apology is trickling into their brains and making its way to their hearts. It might take longer than I thought.

Riley flops her hands against her sides and storms off in the opposite direction.

"Riley!" I race after her. Half the kids at the duck pond look up. "Riley, wait!"

She's moving so fast, I think for a minute that I should just let her go. But then she stops and I nearly knock her over.

"I showed you my meteorite," she says. "I've never shown anyone that before because I didn't want anyone to make fun of me for being so excited about it. And here you were making fun of me the whole time."

"No."

"Yes."

We stand there, Riley breathing hard and fast, the rest of the fair swirling around us: hot dogs, balloons, clowns, and dryer balls. I have nothing more to say except, "I'm so sorry, Riley. I-I'm just not that good at this stuff."

"Obviously." She pulls away from me.

And then I see something over her shoulder. We're standing among rows of easels and canvases at the Science Meets Art exhibit. I walk over to one painting, Riley right behind me, and just as I suspected, there's a smushed *LL* signature at the bottom.

Grandpa must have entered his painting in the exhibit months ago. Why didn't he tell me?

"It's just all brown," Riley says.

She's right; it is all brown, every spot on the canvas. And someone might think that it looks like the work of someone with dementia, someone confused. But I know that brown. Rosebud, mixed with sunray and chestnut.

"Almost looks like chocolate," Riley says. "Like rocky road ice cream."

And maybe Mr. Sid would think it's fresh soil and Dad would think it's a chemical solution bubbling in the lab. But I know it's the color of love and of missing someone. And maybe it doesn't matter about regrets and houses and old cars, because maybe Grandpa's not missing anyone anymore.

And I know how it feels to miss people now, too.

Pumpkin Fest is starting to wind down, vendors

packing up their booths, kids heading back up the hill. The Pumpkin Tournament will start soon on the university fields. The garden tours have probably wrapped up.

"Hey, Riley," I say. "I know a place we can get hot chocolate and crepes. Want to come?"

She crosses her arms again and looks at me, hard.

"It's at my neighbor's house. Mr. Sid. He's a gardener and—"

Riley walks away from me and I stop babbling, watching her climb the hill toward the big tree. When she's at the top she stops, almost like she's waiting for me. And then, instead of turning right at the tree to go home, she turns left.

Toward my neighborhood.

# Thirty-eight

MR. SID IS SITTING among his flowers, grinning and eating a chocolate crepe when Riley and I come by.

"Madeline!" He waves us over, wiping his mouth with a napkin.

"This place is beautiful," Riley says, and of course Mr. Sid beams.

"Help yourself," he says, pointing inside. "Crepes and hot chocolate on the stovetop. Strawberries and bananas next to the fruit bowl."

I'm surprised to find Mom and Dad inside. "We sold out of dryer balls," Mom says. "Had to pack up the booth early this year. Now, that's a first!"

"We were looking all over the festival for you." Dad's wearing a frayed and faded Hawaiian shirt, spooning chocolate over their crepes. "My birthday girl!" he wraps me in a hug, Mom joining in and squeezing the life out of me. Then they give me a thousand kisses, give or take, a birthday tradition from when I was little.

"Get off!" I say, half laughing. "I'm practically a teen-ager!"

I can barely look at Riley when they let me go. "This is Riley, from school," I say.

"Nice to meet you," Dad says, and squirts a dollop of whipped cream into each of our hands. Even though we're in middle school now, we slurp it off.

We all join Mr. Sid in his garden, which glows with white twinkly lights and dragonfly lanterns. Mom starts singing "Happy Birthday," and soon everyone is singing on the little porch. Even Riley.

Nana, Brooke, and Mouse walk over from next door when they hear us, and we have to start all over because Nana wants to sing it in a round. We're laughing so hard because we sound terrible, like a bunch of dogs howling at the moon. Even Bark comes out to investigate, sitting in front of Mr. Sid's gate.

"Second place," Mr. Sid says, holding up his plaque. He must be feeling *really* good, because he throws a piece of crepe over the fence for Bark to gobble up.

Mouse and Bark are sniffing at each other through the gate when I notice a clump of people walking down our quiet street. They're all wearing navy-blue sweatshirts, and there's a giant owl walking behind them. It's the soc-cer team and our mascot, Hoot Hoot.

Dexter's at the lead, and he stops at Mr. Sid's gate. "Brooke?"

Brooke pops up, smoothing down her hair, a look of bewilderment on her face. She trips across the porch and down the front steps.

"Heard you couldn't make the game today," Dexter says, like he's reading a script. He's kind of awkward without a soccer ball. "I want you to have this." Something is balled in his fist.

Brooke takes it, a giddy smile on her face, and shakes it out. It's Dexter's jersey, number 22, with all the grass and dirt stains a girl could want.

"Twenty-two!" the team shouts, making us all jump out of our seats.

"Hoot! Hoot!"

"Thank you." Brooke holds the jersey up for everyone to see. "I — it's — thank you." I've never seen her at a loss for words.

"No big deal," Dexter says, his face going burgundy. "We're having a real after-party this year. Um, next weekend." He hands her an envelope. "Check it out, and if you can make it or whatever, just let me know. See you at school and, you know, at lunch or something."

Brooke just stands there as the soccer team disappears back down the street, Hoot Hoot waddling after them. When they turn the corner, she puts the jersey on over her T-shirt and settles back onto the porch steps, a giant grin on her face. I can tell everyone has questions about the envelope and the after-party invitation, but for now they just let her sip her hot chocolate and relish the moment.

Sitting next to Riley, I'm thinking about a lot of things, like making amends and wishing Grandpa were here, when I notice something about the nearly naked lady. Her hair. It's not just regular brown. More like rosebud, mixed with sunray and chestnut.

I stand up, covering my eyes mostly, because I have a very bad feeling. I step carefully down the front patio and into the garden.

"Madeline?" Mom says. "You okay?"

And there it is, in the bottom right-hand corner. I stagger back and point. "Mom!"

"What?" Nana says, panicked. "Is it a spider? Oh, kill it, Daniel. Kill it!"

"That's Grandpa's signature," I say, flapping my hands toward the canvas. "L-L. L-L!"

Brooke's the first to realize what this means, dropping her cup and sending it clattering down the porch steps. "Ew."

Mom rushes off the porch. "That can't be. It's not even his painting style!"

I point at the small letters again, the rest of the party just standing there, staring. "I've seen his signature a thousand times in his studio," I say, and cover my face completely. "This isn't just a naked painting. It's a naked painting of *Grandma*."

"I'm seriously going to vomit," Brooke says.

Now everyone is up and rushing toward the canvas, Dad tripping over the extension cord and making the lights flicker. Mr. Sid gets there first, pulling the painting off its easel and holding it up for a better look. "Your grandfather painted this? The scientist?"

"He painted in his free time," Dad says. "Never realized how much until the other day."

Mr. Sid puts the painting back on the easel. "Apparently he had some art in his blood."

"But it doesn't look anything like his other paintings," I say.

Mr. Sid shrugs. "Maybe he took a class. Maybe he tried something new. Sometimes it takes a few tries to find your style."

I realize that Riley's still standing there with her hand over her face.

Can't a girl just make a friend without something horrific happening? I mean, Riley's family isn't perfect, and her sisters are bossy, but my family takes the cupcake on weirdness. What kind of family puts a portrait of their mostly naked grandmother out for all to see?

"Will someone *please* cover that thing up?" I say.

Mr. Sid chuckles, turning the painting to face a hedge of shrubbery. Riley takes her hand away from her face, and then she bursts out laughing. I'm so startled, I just stare at her, because honestly, what's so funny about a nearly naked grandmother? Believe me, nothing. Nothing at all.

But apparently everyone thinks it's funny, because soon they're all laughing.

I cross my arms.

But when Mouse and Bark start howling with us, I just can't help it. I laugh so hard I should probably worry about getting a nosebleed.

But tonight is not for worrying. It's for celebrating.

# Thirty-nine

At HOME LATER, after we've decided on birthday cake for breakfast because we're still too full of crepes and chocolate now, I head down to my basement bedroom. I flick on the light and find that my box of things is missing from the top of the dryer. My toothbrush and towel and FUTURE SCIENTIST! cup are gone as well.

I take the stairs two at a time. Brooke is standing in the family room, blowing on her fingernails. "Don't get any ideas. I only moved you back in because you were so pathetic down there."

"I was fine," I lie, wanting to run over and tackle her with a hug. "So, we're going to share a room again?"

"Just keep your creepy science stuff on your side."

"I don't have any more science stuff," I say.

"Nana and I took it out of the trash," Brooke says. "Don't make me regret it."

I try to be cool. I sprint up the stairs and everything looks like it did before I started middle school and before

Brooke moved out. Before I dumped everything into a box and threw it away. Einstein is tacked up over my bed, and Brooke's side is a panda explosion. I peek into my closet laboratory. It's all there.

I'm already snuggled under my blankets in my galaxy pajamas when Brooke comes upstairs. She pushes all of her pandas off her bed and rearranges them at her feet, clicking off the night-light.

"Thank you," I say into the dark. I mean for letting me back into our room and saving my science stuff, but also for pushing me to make a new friend. And to make things right.

I hear her turn over, and I see the outline of her panda wearing a sombrero at the edge of her bed. "I know you did all that stuff for me," she says. "The jersey from Dexter and the party at the planetarium."

"The jersey was all Dexter," I say.

"The party, though," Brooke says. "What was in that envelope was all you. You gave up your private planetarium show."

"My friends and I can go to the planetarium anytime," I say. "We don't need our own private show."

I had Dexter invite the soccer team for a party at the planetarium with the cheerleading squad. An after-after-party for next weekend, when Brooke will be allowed out again. They all said yes. Guess there's a scientist in all of us.

"Maddie," Brooke says, setting her birthday party panda on my nightstand, "you can be pretty cool, you know that?"

Maybe turning twelve is not so bad.

# forty

FALL IS QUICKLY getting its chill, the leaves dulling to brown from their vibrant reds, oranges, and yellows. I place a pair of water skis next to a dusty camping chair. "Who even water skis in this family?" I say.

Brooke shakes her head, inspecting a pair of old placemats. She holds up one with a gaping hole in the middle. "Those things will eat anything."

She claims she found a spider cricket munching on a cotton ball one night in the basement. But I looked it up. Spider crickets are neither radioactive nor alien, and they prefer a diet of other insects rather than cotton balls and placemats from 1974. They're also called camelback crickets. Mom finally broke down and let Dad call an exterminator.

"Toss it," I say, pointing to an overflowing garbage bag by the brick wall.

Bark lumbers up the road, stopping to smell our Yard Sale sign and a pile of old beach towels. I pull out my

swabs because lately I've been reading about the antibacterial properties of dog slobber.

"What are you doing?" Brooke says.

"Hey, Bark, look!" I say, holding out one of Dad's Fris-
bees from college. As soon as Bark comes over to investigate, I swab his jowls. I'm so fast he barely notices, but
when I try for a second swipe, he bites down and trots
back home with a swab hanging out of his mouth.

"You are so strange," Brooke says. "I'll pretend I didn't
just see that happen."

"There is nothing strange in the name of science!"

I go back into the house and down into the basement,
where Mom and Dad are sorting their junk. Mom has a
broken box in her hand. "Evelyn," Dad's saying. "You never
know when you might need that."

"What is it?" I say.

"A wine-making kit." Mom pushes it into my arms.
"Now run and mark it for twenty-five cents!"

I drop the kit on the long table in the driveway and
reposition the Yard Sale sign on our gate. A pair of roller
skates hangs from the fence, and I place them on the table, marking them FREE! because who knows what's living
in those things, and also they're Dad's from high school.
Maybe a museum will buy them.

All I know is that everything that's not essential has

to go if we want to convert the basement to a real room. We're going to use some of the money from the sale of Grandpa's house. Brooke and I don't know what we'll use the extra room for yet. A bedroom, maybe. Or a hangout place. Either way, I've already hung up the HOME IS WHERE YOU LIGHT YOUR BUNSEN BURNER sign over the door next to Brooke's PANDA CROSSING sign.

Before the sale gets under way, I run up to my room to quickly organize my orders for the day. Three SOPs: *How to Ask Your Mom if You Can Go to the Movies with a Boy. How to Eat a Bag of Cheetos Without Getting Orange Fingers. How to Win Over Your Teacher.*

After my lab notebook became public knowledge and nearly ruined my life, Dexter had asked me to write him an SOP on *How to Stop Your Teammates from Stealing Your Water Bottle and Hiding It in the Ball Bag.* I said no way. My SOP-writing days were over. But then he said he'd swab the inside of his soccer locker for me, and it was pretty much an offer I couldn't pass up in the name of science.

Soon I was writing procedures on *How to Get Out of Sprints During Practice* and *How to Make Friends with Your Coach* for the rest of the soccer team. Word spread through school, and ever since I've been helping kids out of sticky situations, one SOP at a time.

I put each SOP into a separate folder and head back downstairs.

Dad comes outside and checks everything on the extra table with Grandpa's stuff on it. There were a few things that didn't make it into the U-Haul that we're willing to try to sell again. The science museum is buying Grandpa's house. They're going to fix it up and make it into a library and a place for special exhibits so that important scientists like Grandpa will always be remembered. They said they'll give me a member card so I can come whenever I want. They're going to keep his leather couch in the attic and hang up some of his paintings. Elizabeth and I already decided we're going to study there after school instead of at the library.

Abby is walking up the road in front of our house, Bark at her heels. I pull out the folder with my SOP on *How to Ask Your Mom if You Can Go to the Movies with a Boy* and hand it to her when she comes through the gate. "Be careful with step two, okay? You have to really mean it, or she'll catch on right away," I say.

Brooke's right behind me. She grabs the folder. "Are you serious? You're asking my little sister for advice?"

Abby shrugs. "It's called a standard operating procedure, Brooke. Everyone's using them."

"Step one," Brooke reads. "Wait until the sink is really full and then say, 'I got this, Mom!' and wash the dishes." She looks at me. "Not bad. Step two." She clears her throat. "Tell her that 'insert boy's name' is having a sleepover party on Saturday and his parents might not be home but it's okay because his brother in college will be there with all of his friends." Brooke laughs. "That's not going to happen." She continues reading. "Step three. Once your mother has stopped freaking out, ask her if it's okay if you and the boy just go to the movies instead." Brooke hands Abby the folder. "Well, maybe she gives good advice on this one little topic."

So far nobody from the lunch table has asked me for advice. Once I almost wrote an SOP for Amy: *How to Carry Six Encyclopedias at One Time,* with a diagram and everything. But I decided to save it in a drawer. Even though they've been letting me sit at their table lately, it might take more time for their hearts to warm all the way up to me again.

"So much for not writing SOPs anymore," Brooke says.

I shrug. "I tell everyone who wants one that sometimes science doesn't even work. No guarantee."

I write a new SOP in my head: *How to Handle a Middle School Situation When the SOP Fails.*

*Step 1. Remain calm.*

*Step 2. Take a break. (Visit the brain at the science museum. Eat a Three Sisters cupcake. Be kind to someone.)*

*Step 3. Try again. Maybe a different way.*

Bark trots off to greet someone walking down the street. It's Riley this time. I called her earlier and told her I had something for her.

I grab the burned-out beaker from Grandpa's table and run to meet her.

# A NOTE FROM THE AUTHOR

I was first introduced to Von Willebrand disease (VWD) in 2006 while working in a research lab. Approximately 1 percent of the U.S. population has VWD, making it the most common bleeding disorder, and yet not many people have heard of it. It is most often inherited, and although the symptoms are usually mild, as it is for Maddie and her father, the disease can range in severity. For more information, visit www.hemophilia.org.

Infinite thanks and hugs to . . .

My super-agent Marie Lamba, who is warm and kind and knows how to whip a book into shape. Thank you for helping make all of this a reality.

The team at Houghton Mifflin Harcourt for making this book into something so beautiful, and especially to Jeannette Larson. It has been a dream working with such an incredible editor.

Jeanette Cesta for her expert guidance on all things VWD. Thank you for being so generous with your time and answering my countless questions.

My writers group of more than ten years: Ellen Braaf,

Valerie Patterson, Lezlie Evans, Lorrie-Ann Melnick, Corey Wetzel, and Sydney Dunlap. They are wholly responsible for my perseverance through rejections and revisions.

The Society of Children's Book Writers and Illustrators, especially the Mid-Atlantic region. I am so grateful to be a part of such a supportive and welcoming community.

My family (from the New Englanders to the Midwesterners to the Philadelphians) for your love and encouragement.

My mom, who provides endless mom-character ideas (all good, of course), and my dad, who took me to New York as a teenager and showed me what it looked like to be a real writer (hence my departure into science). To Devin for my healthy fear of bugs, and Kara and Cailin for being the best kind of sisters.

Jaeda and Caden for loving libraries and bookstores and book-nooks just as much as I do, and teaching me how to utilize every window of opportunity to write (even if the window is only open for ten minutes and it's still a bit loud and mostly wrecks the house and requires chocolate milk and peanut butter waffles).

And of course to Jay, who told everyone I was a writer even when I wasn't yet, and who set his own dreams aside and went to work every day in a suit while I pursued my dreams at home, mostly in my pajamas.